I0633411

The Allington Collection

CLEAN REGENCY ROMANCE

THE LADY SERIES

DAISY LANDISH

Editing by Rachael Lammie
Cover art by CharmingPixyArt

BEACHES AND TRAILS
PUBLISHING

About the Author

Daisy Landish is a romance and contemporary fiction author living in the UK, whose clean and sweet novellas have tugged at readers' heartstrings across the pond and beyond. When she's not writing love stories, Daisy spends her time reading, hiking at dawn, and riding into the sunset on her horse, Rosebud.

www.daisylandishromance.com

facebook.com/daisylandishromance

x.com/daisy_landish

instagram.com/daisylandishbooks

amazon.com/author/daisylandish

bookbub.com/authors/daisy-landish

goodreads.com/Daisy_Landish

Also by Daisy Landish

Clean Regency Romance

The Lady Series - The Allington Collection

The Lady Series - The Gillingham Collection

The Lady Series - The Blackmore Collection

The Lady Series - The Norrington Collection

Clean Contemporary Romance

Maplewood Grove Series

Love on Spruce Island

Second Chance

Cherry Tree Island

The Wedding Trio

Extra Credit

Counting on the Cowboy

Focusing on the Cowboy

Mistletoe Magic

Grounded at Christmas

Cozy Mysteries

Sophie Brooks Mysteries

Jane and Kennedy Daniels Mysteries

Pine Grove Mysteries

Annie Archer Paranormal Mysteries

Wilma Wade Holiday Mysteries

Mike and Maddie Mysteries

Mystic Moonhaven Mysteries

Sweater Weather: Cozy Mysteries for Fall

Summer Vibes: Cozy Mysteries for Summer
Let it Snow: Cozy Mysteries for Winter
Spring Break: Cozy Mysteries for Spring

Taming The Lady

THE LADY SERIES BOOK ONE

CHAPTER 1

Josephina

J osephina knew that she was a disappointment to her family as well as an embarrassment. Still, she did not give a tinker's whit.

She did, however, care enough not to use this expression aloud in society. Josephina loathed having to take a maid with her every time she left the house. If a maid was not immediately in her sights, she did occasionally venture out alone. She drove both a curricle and a barouche and rode faster than ladies should. Discussing the mode, and any number of other silly things ladies were supposed to talk about, was something that bored her to death. She kept abreast of the latest news and would have loved to discuss loftier matters, but those were not topics for a Lady to discuss.

Josephina believed she should have been born a man. As far as she was concerned, the strictures attached to being a Lady were a load of fudge. Gentlemen could do as they wished, not so for ladies. The acceptable pursuits of ladies held no interest for her. There was no greater torture than to spend the day choosing a ball gown. She had yet to find a bonnet that could be secured tightly enough not to blow away at the slightest breeze. As for a reticule, more often than not, she would set it down somewhere and forget about it. If she lost it at home, it often took most of the household to locate it, earning her another dressing-down from her mother. If she lost it elsewhere, it was her father that would be displeased.

At the age of four and twenty, Josephina remained unmarried. As the eldest girl in the household, she was expected to marry well. She had refused a gaggle of suitors she did not feel were up to snuff. Her mother called her an old maid, a girl on the shelf. She did not mind it overmuch. It was far better than handing her life away to any of the men who had offered for her. Better to be past her prime than to spend life with a man she did not love.

Josephina had three sisters and a younger brother. Camilla, older by a year, was married to the Hon. Tobias Wimpole. He was a foppish, Pink of the Ton who spent more time on his necktie and multicoloured waistcoats than anything else, including his wife. Clarissa, a strait-laced, prudish girl four years her junior, had recently agreed to accept the first offer she had received. A mistake as far as Josephina was concerned.

An eleven-year gap had produced two more siblings: her brother Jackson (her favourite) and Sophia, who were eleven-year-old twins.

Josephina and Camilla were close. But she seldom saw her sister who had moved to another county after the wedding. Clarissa, however, disapproved of everything Josephina did and made no secret of it. As a result, they were not too fond of each other. As for Jackson and Sophia, she adored them. And they too worshipped their outlandish sister.

She was grateful that she had no older brother intent on shepherding her everywhere and taking their parents' side. As it was, her parents were firmly convinced she should set an example for the others by settling down. Josephina was equally convinced she need not bother. Her unmarried sister had already secured a husband, and the twins, who were tough, young, and unimpressionable, didn't care if she kicked up a lark and had a little fun.

Lord and Lady Barrington gave up on marrying their daughter when Josephina refused her latest suitor, the extremely eligible, though slightly older, Duke of Barclay. This was on the heels of her rejecting the perfectly acceptable Captain Billings. Lord and Lady Barrington thought her refusal of the Duke to be entirely unfounded. She felt the Duke was too old, but he was only one and fifty. Captain Billings, who she had assessed as tediously dull, would be away most of the time. To her mind, an early death would be preferable to spending a lifetime in such company.

There had been no lack of suitors in her first Season. The gentlemen were simply not up to the mark. Not that they were unsuitable, but Josephina was just unwilling to marry. She enjoyed the flirtations for a while, but they were unequal to the vexation of later having to listen to a proposal she was going to refuse. Generally, she found gentlemen did not take refusal well. She would spend an uncomfortable half-hour soothing their ruffled feathers, making assurances that it was all her fault. Thankfully, most suitors were sufficiently embarrassed or offended to desist immediately. She could not have tolerated having any of them approach her father after a refusal. To avoid being called a heartless flirt, she decided to keep them all at bay and discourage any signs of courtship early on whenever she could.

Even Josephina's critics called her a handsome woman. Her figure, although she loosened her corset every chance she got, was pleasing and well proportioned. Neither dainty nor too sturdy. Her face was deemed attractive. Despite her unruly red hair, she had a lovely complexion. Sharp green eyes held a glint of mischief and hid a keen sense of observation.

Like a cat, Josephina didn't miss a thing. This trait did not appeal to most gentlemen who required a Lady's undivided attention. These young men said nothing that would keep Josephina in rapture. Though she turned heads in a ball gown, the only attire that genuinely suited her was her riding habit. She had taken great pains in selecting the cut, the fabric, and the fasteners, thus making the garment as comfortable as was fashionably possible.

Sitting on a horse, she looked like a goddess. She felt free and powerful, both of which she was denied in other parts of her life. She adored horses and had always felt a kinship with the four-legged beasts. They shared a special bond. She could communicate with horses, even horses that belonged to other people. If not held tightly, most horses would gravitate around her. Horsemanship was not considered a ladylike pursuit. True, ladies were congratulated on their riding abilities. But they were not expected to have extensive knowledge on the matter.

Mores was the pity, for that was indeed Josephina's favourite topic of conversation.

All the eligible bachelors found her appearance, behaviour, and aloofness to be an irresistible combination. Each was certain they could tame her, and it had not occurred to any of them that she should not be tamed.

Unable to suffer the confinements that society tried to impose on Josephina, she did what she wanted, within reason. This included going for long walks in the park with her cat, who would follow faithfully behind, stopping the odd time to climb a tree. Some would call her eccentric. Galloping through the park or driving her curricle at high speed had earned Josephina the reputation of enjoying raising a breeze - not a pleasant trait for a Lady of quality. Her family were not notable enough for her to get away with such comportment. Some thought her too haughty, but as she had set her cap at no one, she was considered harmless.

One morning, Josephina's mother received word that her dear sister was ill. She immediately started preparations to leave for the country, likely taking Clarissa and Sophia for company. Lord Barrington wanted Josephina to stay and keep house for him. His time would be better spent at his club than with his sister-in-law. Usually, Josephina would object. However, as Jackson would also stay behind to keep up with his studies, her time at home would be more enjoyable than in the country. She made a show of protest, lest her mother think her too keen on staying home.

A morning of shopping ensued, as Lady Barrington insisted that she must purchase crucial items before leaving civilisation. Josephina was to accompany her, and in the interest of getting rid of one of her parents, she agreed.

Her mother, expecting a refusal, was in good spirits on the drive to Town. Josephina decided it was the perfect time to broach a matter she had been thinking of for some time.

"Mama, I do not care for the name Josephina. It sounds old and decrepit. Wasn't I named after one of your deceased aunts? I'd prefer to be called Joe, or Josie, a lively person's name," she ventured, regarding her parent with a smiling countenance. "But Josephina, you *are* old," said her mother. "Mama, I am four and twenty. That's not old," she replied.

"Your sister is nineteen and will be married before she is twenty," came her mother's reply. Since her sister's engagement, Lady Barrington had used this argument to try and force Josephina to reconsider the Duke's offer. He had assured her that he would give Josephina time to see the validity of his proposal.

"Yes, because she is a silly goose," retorted Josephina. "Josephina!" shouted her mother, appalled. "James is such a bore, Mama," she continued.

"The Hon. James Farringdon is not a bore. He is a fine young man, and your sister was lucky to receive his offer," replied her mother haughtily.

"What fustian! Clarissa is a simpleton to marry him. He is a penny-pinching fusspot and fastidious to a fault. He will make her life a misery," Josephina insisted.

"You are mistaken, and your attitude is the reason you remain on the shelf. I refuse to call you anything but your name. Your father and I chose it carefully, and you shall wear it with honour! Besides, it is unbecoming to shorten your name like a commoner. Now, I will hear no more talk of this nonsense. Nor will I hear any disparaging remarks about your sister's future husband," she said in a huff, quickly smoothing out the frown that had appeared on her brow.

Josephina was forced to drop the matter and attend to fabric, bonnets and the like for the next endless hours. She was looking forward to a spirited ride on Dark Knight when she arrived home, but it was too late. A quick visit at the stables assured her that John, her groom and devoted servant, had everything ready for the following day. When asked if he had received word from her best friend, Arabella, she was told that Miss Allington would meet her as arranged.

CHAPTER 2

Hint of a Scandal

Josephina awoke the following morning with only one thought in her head: joining the hunt. She had managed this feat a few times in the past, but it was never easy. There were so many things that needed to happen with such precision that it often seemed impossible.

The evening before, Lord Barrington had told the cook that he would be spending the day at his club once the family had departed. She had to figure out when he would arise and when he would leave.

Josephina had heard the carriage leave sometime earlier for the countryside. Jackson was a trustworthy accomplice; she had helped him out of so many scrapes that she knew he would go along with any scheme, for her sake.

While her maid fetched her breakfast, Josephina donned her riding habit and dressed her own hair. Arriving with the tray, her maid tsked at her but said nothing. She would have objected even if Josephina had a proper outing.

As it was, she looked perfectly respectable for a morning ride. Before the maid left, Josephina asked about her father and brother. The maid informed her that her father was still abed and that Jackson was in the garden with the dogs.

Josephina downed her tea and took a bite of toast. She was too excited to eat and soon went in search of her brother. They sat together for a while as she told him about her plans for joining the hunt. When the tutor came to fetch him, she went back into the house, just as her father headed into the breakfast room.

"You've been out already?" he asked as a footman brought him a plate of eggs and a cup of tea.

"Not yet, Papa. Shall I join you for a cup of tea before I leave?" she asked.

"I don't want to keep you from your morning exercise," said the Lord with a dismissive wave. She kissed her father's cheek and left him to his morning paper.

She walked briskly to the stables, intent on leaving before anyone and noticed John's attire. She'd needed to purchase John's help and silence. He would be held accountable should anything happen to her. The only way to ensure her safety was to accompany her on the hunt. She'd had to use her own money to have John outfitted as a gentleman for the hunt.

They met Arabella and her groom, who conveniently, was John's nephew, and the four of them made their way to the meet.

It was a clear, crisp morning, perfect for a hunt. What made it less than perfect was the appearance of two ladies in their elegant riding habits. Ladies were not usually invited to hunts, let alone one this early in the morning. As it was unclear who had invited them, the polite thing to do was to include them. This was the exact outcome Josephina and Arabella had hoped for. Had either of their fathers been in attendance, they would have been sent home immediately. This was not a social engagement. No introductions were made, and the ladies were able to maintain their anonymity. The gentlemen would simply ignore them.

While they waited for the hunt to begin, the two friends passed the time discussing the horses of the other hunters. It was their love of horses that had brought Josephina and Arabella together a few years previously. They were also in agreement in their mutual loathing of ladylike things such as shopping for ball gowns.

A footman was presenting the stirrup cups on a silver tray. There had been a commotion to find a suitable drink for two ladies, as their presence had not been expected. Luckily, a bottle of fortified wine was fetched, and the matter was resolved.

The gentlemen were discussing their horses, recent hunts, and the two young ladies. Josephina and Arabella, oblivious to their attention, stood apart from the men to have their own lively discussion.

"It's a shame that Lady Beauford no longer comes out. No one frowned at us when she was here, but I understand the dear Lady is rather on in years and finds it too difficult," Arabella said.

"Indeed. Being in the presence of a married Lady was preferable. Alas, it seems we are destined to remain alone in this venture," Josephina replied.

"Did I tell you my brother is coming home today? You will like him. You might even consider him a suitable match. Can you imagine it? We could be sisters!" Arabella said excitedly.

"I hoped to be home when he arrived," Arabella continued. "But as he gave no indication of his arrival time, I didn't want to miss the hunt. Mother has a headache and was still abed when I rose. I could not let the occasion pass," she finished in a rush as the hunters started to move. As they followed, Josephina recalled why Arabella's brother had been away for a few years.

Frederick was forced to go abroad after engaging in a duel that could have been avoided. One cannot overlook a slight to one's sister. Frederick had found Anthony Barlow, a young man from a good family, attempting to steal a kiss from an unwilling Prunella. It would have been a simple thing to pull the young man and request an apology. However, as Frederick grabbed his arm, the man became incensed and started yelling invectives.

Frederick had pushed Anthony into the shrubbery to avoid a squirmish that would have alerted others to the situation. When the man righted himself, Frederick demanded that he take his attentions elsewhere. The stupid young pup took offence at being so accosted and insisted on satisfaction. The ensuing duel was a nasty business.

They had met at dawn and drew their weapons. Everyone knew that you were meant to shoot wide. No one got hurt, and everyone's honour was restored. However, just as they fired, they heard shouts that the Constable was coming. In looking over, Frederick aimed a little too far to the left and managed to shoot poor Anthony in the arm. It was only a graze; Anthony would make a full recovery. But as duelling was illegal, Frederick had to make himself scarce until the commotion died down.

"Well, Arabella, we should enjoy this hunt as it may be our last. With an older brother in residence, one that likely hunts, I doubt we'll get away with such unladylike behaviour while he is near. It won't hurt my reputation. I was firmly established as a twit when I refused the Duke of Barclay. Yours, however, remains unblemished. If you continue to associate with me, you might be deemed guilty by association," Josephina warned her friend.

"Josephina! You are my dearest friend. I would not cease our friendship for all the Dukes and Earls in England. Besides, I do not care a fig about society, but I do want to see Freddie. I hope he is there when I get home. Will you ride home with me to meet him?" Arabella was even more excited at this new idea.

"I do not think that would be the best time to meet your wayward brother. I expect your mother and siblings have been anticipating him as ardently as you have. It should be an intimate reunion," she replied.

"Yes, of course, you are right. But I must introduce you. Frederick is a real Nonesuch." Arabella was not going to give up.

"Indeed? I must meet him immediately," Josephina laughed. "I have heard of such men. There is a Corinthian in my acquaintance, but I have never met a real Nonesuch!"

"Make fun of me all you wish. You will see," and Arabella left it at that, as they galloped across open land towards a high hedge, where talking became difficult.

Both ladies met it perfectly and sailed over in elegance and grace. On the other side, everyone was waiting while the hounds picked up the scent. Josephina and Arabella sat apart from the rest, observing the spectacle. A distinguished-looking gentleman was riding in their direction.

"Little sister, I had not thought to see you here today. I was under the impression you were having a gentle ride in the country," and he raised his eyebrows in question, a smile on his lips.

"Oh, Freddie," Arabella beamed and reached a hand out to rest on her brother's sleeve.

"I must say, I was terribly impressed with that last fence. If you keep up that level of equestrianship, I will not say anything about you coming out today. However, you must let me accompany you," stated Fredrick.

"Freddie, let me introduce my good friend Lady Josephina Barrington," she paused as Frederick inclined his head. He could neither bow nor take her hand sitting atop a horse.

"May I introduce Frederick Allington, seventh Earl of Sunningdale," she continued, smiling at them both. Josephina gave a demure nod. They exchanged the usual pleasantries but were quickly called back to the task at hand. The other hunters were racing off.

Watching Frederick, Josephina had to agree with her friend's assessment. He sat upon his steed perfectly; his clothes were immaculate and obviously expensive (but not too foppish). The gentleman was most extraordinarily good looking.

The Earl of Sunningdale had similar thoughts about Josephina. Decked in an emerald-green habit with gold piping, fiery red hair curling in the wind, she was striking. What impressed him most was that she was likely the best rider at the hunt, himself included. He was very taken with her horse as well.

CHAPTER 3

Fateful Dinner Party

Meanwhile, Arabella congratulated herself on a job well done. She had managed the introductions. Now they needed to interact in society. It couldn't be a ball, as Josephina could not attend in the absence of her mother. Besides, the Allingtons would steer Frederick away from Josephina, whom they deemed unsuitable. They didn't understand that it was often Josephina who kept Arabella from doing something that would be considered too scandalous.

Prunella, her older sister, was thankfully away at this time. Her husband was spending a year in France overseeing business interests there. When they returned in two months, she would be too late to foil Arabella's plans. Josephina and Frederick would, hopefully, be already betrothed!

On the ride home, Arabella told her brother how sorry she was that her dear friend had to remain at home while her mother was away in the country. The Earl understood her meaning perfectly. He could not pay Josephine a call until she had a suitable chaperone. He would need to contrive a way to see her again.

There had been no pressure to find a wife during the year of mourning after his father's passing. But now that he was home, his mother would have him attend every ball, dinner party, and assembly. If he could avoid the marriage mart entirely, he would consider it a personal victory. He had no intention of entering into a marriage of convenience. He wanted a wife he would enjoy spending time with. Josephina was beautiful and intelligent, but not a bluestocking, and most importantly, she had spirit.

He'd heard of Josephina's antics in the letters he'd received while he was away. She may have pushed the rules of etiquette but had not yet broken them. As a gentleman of good breeding, flush in the pockets and an Earl to boot, he could do as he please. Ladies did not have such a luxury. Josephina was simply wielding what little power was afforded to her, and he rather admired her for it.

After changing his attire, he sent his man to find out as much as possible about Lord Barrington. After luncheon with his family, the valet came back with his report. The man in question spent many afternoons at his club. Frederick hadn't been to White's since before the duel. It was time to make an appearance.

Some of his old acquaintances were glad to see him, but a few stayed clear. This gave him pause. Though he did not consider Josephina to be unsuitable in the least, she may not feel the same about him. He was sure Arabella had told her the whole story. If his sister was right, Josephina would not care a whit about the old scandal.

Lord Barrington was sitting alone, reading a book. Frederick asked if any of his friends could introduce them. He could introduce himself, but it was best to have a mutual acquaintance to add to his credibility, especially with a scandal looming over him.

Lord Barrington was either unaware or unconcerned with his reputation. He invited Frederick to sit and have a drink with him. Frederick mentioned that Arabella and Josephina were friends and that he'd chanced upon them this morning as they were riding. Once their mutual interests were established, they spent a delightful afternoon.

Josephina regaled Jackson with tales of the hunt over luncheon. Their father was still at the club, and they could dodge the tutor to spend some extra time down by the pond. She spent the afternoon reading in the shade, enjoying the blissful silence of her family's absence. She was humming to herself as she entered through the kitchen to speak to the cook about dinner. She was informed that her father had made arrangements and that he was expecting two guests for dinner. How odd, she thought. "Do you know who the guests are?" she asked.

"No, miss," replied the cook as she went back to kneading dough for a pied.

"Do you know if Jackson will be joining us?" she asked.

"Yes, miss," replied the cook without looking up.

Well then, she thought as she left the kitchen, if Jackson was included in the party, indeed, these were not important guests.

Josephina took no particular pains in dressing for dinner. Her father's friends were old and only talked about boxing and investments. They would ignore her and Jackson entirely. She wore one of her plainer gowns and had the maid gather her curls with a simple ribbon. So long as she was presentable, no one in attendance would fault her attire. She was, after all, an old maid.

Josephina and Jackson waited in the drawing-room for the guests to arrive. When Hobson, the butler, showed them in, she was speechless. There stood Arabella and her dashing brother. She was saved from embarrassment when her father entered the room.

"Welcome, welcome," he said as he kissed Arabella's hand and shook Fredrick's. He excused himself as he had Hobson prepare their drinks.

"Arabella, how lovely to see you. Do forgive my casual attire. I thought father had invited some fuddy-duddies from the club," said Josephina, clutching her friend's hands. "Perhaps I should change..." she trailed. Turning to the Earl, she saw a smile on his lips.

"How fetching you look, Miss Barrington. Please do not feel you need to change our account. Are we not among friends?" he said.

"Do not make fun of me, Sir. I am quite embarrassed as it is, " she replied, her eyes downcast.

The Earl took her hand and kissed it.

"I assure you my compliment was most sincere."

The men moved to talk near the fireplace, and Josephina was able to study her guest. He was even more wondrous in evening attire; his top-boots polished to perfection, the cut of his coat adding elegance to his already impressive stature, and the arrangement of his cravat interesting, but not frivolous.

Josephina regretted not taking more time on her appearance. She should have listened to her mother. For the first time, she understood the importance of always looking one's best.

Frederick was tall and well built. He had no need for the padded shoulders or padded calves that some men wore to enhance themselves. Living in a warmer climate for some years had given him a perpetual tan - just a light dusting of gold, so attractive in a man and so unbecoming in a woman. His blonde hair was sun-kissed, and the overall effect was dramatic.

Large chestnut eyes fringed with long lashes had held her gaze as he kissed her hand. Had it not been for his exile, he would have been the man in every mama's mire. She would never have had a chance with such a catch. It seemed luck was on her side.

Dinner was a surprise in more ways than one. In her mother's absence, Josephina saw her father in a new light. Usually, he was quiet and dull, taking little part in the conversation. He was animated and lively with the Earl. He even included Josephina in their exchanges, asking for her opinion. It was a remarkable transformation and an enjoyable evening.

After dessert, Jackson was sent to bed, the gentleman settled to their port and cigars in the study, and the ladies removed to the drawing-room. Josephina has been dying to know how this blessed event had come about.

According to Arabella, Frederick had chanced upon Lord Barrington at White's and been invited to dinner. There was no other information to be had. Regardless, the friends were pleased to have this time alone together.

Lord Barrington was no fool. After he met the Earl at the club, he immediately set a plan in motion. Had his wife been here, she would have likely driven the Earl away in a maddening attempt to push Josephina on him. And he was sure Josephina would have refused to consider him simply because he was her mother's choice.

Lord Barrington may be a quiet man, but he knew his family members intimately. Mother and daughter were more alike than they cared to acknowledge; stubborn and unyielding, both. Lord Barrington saw an opportunity when the Earl mentioned he was looking for horses for his new phaeton.

"Lord Allington, my daughter is an excellent judge of horseflesh. I'm sure she could be of assistance on this matter."

Frederick nearly choked on his port. This was far too easy. He was almost giddy at the prospect of spending an afternoon discussing horses with the young lady. "I shall accompany you both, of course," the older man added.

"Of course, Sir," replied Fredrick, only moderately disappointed.

They made plans to meet after luncheon on the morrow. With the matter settled, they joined the ladies in the drawing-room sporting matching smiles of victory.

Once the guests had departed, Lord Barrington informed Josephina of the plans he'd made. Her eyes were like saucers. She didn't know what surprised her most: being praised for her equestrianship or the unorthodox outing he had arranged.

"Before you get too excited, Josephina, your presence is only in a consulting capacity. I forbid you to take the reigns of the phaeton and drive the horses yourself. Don't think I haven't seen you racing down the street when you thought I was at the club," he said, wagging a finger at her.

Josephina could not help smiling even as her father reprimanded her. She thought she heard a touch of pride in his voice. She bowed her head and replied, "Yes, Sir", as meekly as she could manage.

Before retiring, Josephina asked if Jackson could accompany them, as it would be educational for the lad. Her father agreed, and they good-night. Josephina all but flew to her rooms in joyful expectation of the morrow. She had no idea how she would find sleep.

CHAPTER 4
Equiestrianship, Indeed!

The Earl brought his younger brother, Henry, as a companion for Jackson. So, a large party went to look at the horses. The Earl was himself an excellent judge of horseflesh and did not really need another opinion. Still, it had seemed like a perfect excuse to spend some time in Josephina's company. Having seen her ride, he appreciated the magnificence of her mount, and her opinion would prove valuable.

Once their task had been dispatched, Frederick had his groom fetch the picnic he had arranged for the occasion. They found a lovely spot in the park, under the shade of a large Oak tree.

There was a lot of space for the two young boys to run around, and Frederick had thought to bring along a kite to entertain them and keep them out of trouble.

Arabella engaged Lord Barrington in conversation so that Josephina and Frederick could have a moment to speak on their own. She made up some story about wanting him to help her ascertain the type of bird perched on a nearby tree.

The Earl seized the opportunity to discuss what appeared to be Josephina's favourite topic: horses. They had a lively discussion, and Arabella and Lord Barrington were back to join them all too soon. It was getting late. The boys were called back, and everyone exclaimed it had been the best outing and the best picnic.

"Lord Barrington," said the Earl as they were parting company," won't you and your daughter join us for dinner on Friday at Sunnydale?"

"Yes, of course. We'd be delighted," came the Lord's quick response.

The girls embraced and winked at one another. Things were going so well!

When they arrived home, Jackson asked if he could have a private word with Josephina. Alarmed by the solemnness of his request, she suggested they take a walk through the grounds.

When they were some distance from the house, Josephina asked her brother what was bothering him.

"When I was playing with Henry today, he told me something most upsetting," the boy stared. Josephina nodded, encouraging him to go on.

"He told me in strict confidence. But as he needs help, I knew I had to tell you."

"Of course, I'll help in any way I can, Jack," she soothed.

"It seems he placed a wager on something or other and lost. As he has no money to pay the debt, the other boy is threatening to tell his parents about Arabella and you attending today's hunt."

"How does he know about that?" she asked.

"The boy is Philip James, Duke Simmon's younger brother."

The Duke had been at the hunt that day.

"How much was the bet?" asked Josephina, who was surprised to hear it was a relatively large sum.

"I am afraid I am a little purse-pinched until the end of the month when I get my pin money. Would it do then?"

"I'm afraid not. If the money is not paid by midday tomorrow, Philip says he will directly send word to Lady Allington. There will be the devil to pay if she finds out about Arabella."

"Yes, I can see that. What about Frederick? I'm sure he would help," she suggested.

"He barely knows his brother and is afraid he'll be scolded for being so irresponsible. And he won't tell Arabella as she may worry or feel guilty on his behalf."

"Let me see what I can manage, and I will tell you in the morning."

Josephina had no idea how to manage such a sum. She couldn't ask her father for it. Eventually, she decided there was only one thing to do. She had to tell Frederick.

She dispatched a quick note to Arabella saying she would be calling on her tomorrow morning. Hopefully, Arabella would find a way to include her brother. She also wrote a letter to slip to Frederick, should they not have an opportunity to speak privately.

In the end, it was all relatively simple. Happily, Lady Allington, Countess of Sunningdale, and her other daughters were out when Josephina arrived. While she and Arabella were visiting in the sitting room, Frederick came in to see his sister. He seemed genuinely surprised but happy to see Josephina. The meeting had not been pre-arranged, a happy coincidence.

Moments later, the tea tray came in, and Arabella took a moment to speak with the maid. Josephina whispered, "Lord Allington. I have a matter of some urgency to discuss with you. It's about your brother, Henry."

Frederick raised an eyebrow. He was intrigued.

"Before I explain, you must promise not to be cross with the lad," she continued. He narrowed his eyes and nodded. Josephina quickly relayed the information that Jackson had told her.

"Indeed, that is most vexing. I shall summon Henry immediately," replied the Earl.

"Perhaps you could give me the money, and the boys could figure it out among themselves?" she suggested.

"Absolutely not. If Henry gives in to blackmail, we'll never hear the end of this. Trust me, I know exactly what to do," he said. The maid had gone, and Arabella was pouring the tea.

"Will you join us, brother?" she asked.

"I'm afraid not. My apologies, ladies, I have urgent business to attend to," he said.

With a bow, he left the sitting room. Josephina hoped she had done the right thing.

When she arrived home, Jackson was waiting for her. Henry was upset with Jackson for breaking his confidence. The Earl had gone with Henry to meet Philip James. He'd been so fearsome that the lad had apologised and promised never to make such threats again. The matter had been resolved, and the brothers had grown closer.

When the Countess of Sunningdale heard that Josephina and her father were coming for dinner, she was most displeased. She explained to her son that she wanted her daughter kept away from that sort of company.

Frederick was highly annoyed and asked his mother to expand on the matter. The Countess answered that Josephina's morals were not all they should be. Frederick was furious and reminded his mother that she remained at Sunningdale Hall at his discretion. He told her that if she was unhappy with his choices, perhaps it would be better to remove herself to the Dowager's cottage in the country.

Most put out by this idea, she quickly tried to justify her words by explaining that she was only thinking of her daughter's future. He let her talk for a while until she finally offered to arrange a sumptuous dinner, at which point he simply asked, "You will be gracious and welcome my guests?"

"Of course. I am always a gracious host," she replied, clearly affronted.

"Let me be plain. Suppose your behaviour in any way makes Josephina feel uncomfortable. In that case, you may find somewhere else to live," he added and stalked out of the room.

His mother had always been a cold, distant woman with rigid convictions of what she believed was right. She had made his father's life miserable, and Frederick would never forgive her for that. His father had been a wonderful man who had done his best to protect the children from her strict rules. It was apparent that the Countess didn't like children. She'd done her duty, produced an heir and a spare. It was unfortunate that she'd given birth to two daughters before Henry came along. But that's what governesses were for.

It was the Countess who had insisted that Frederick leave the country, telling him he was ruining his sister's chances of a good marriage if he stayed. His father had said it would blow over and just to wait a few weeks. But the Countess refused to have Prunella's first Season tarnished by the scandal.

It seemed he'd made the right choice in leaving. Prunella met and married George, a man she loved. While she and George travelled to France, Frederick had stayed with the newlyweds and gotten to know his new brother-in-law.

They had a lovely time together, and Frederick could not wait for the couple to come home. Prunella had changed since being married. She was kinder and more open-minded. Frederick hoped his sisters would mend their relationship and that Prunella would be as enamoured with Josephina as he was.

CHAPTER 5

Surprise Visitor

W hile sitting at his desk in the welcome silence of the study, Frederick recollected one of his last conversations with the previous Earl. His father had advised against marrying for money or consequence. He told him that when he met the right woman, he would know instantly. He had, however, cautioned his son to take his time to be sure that the woman he loved was really all that she appeared to be. It seemed that Frederick's mother had been less than transparent during their courtship.

He was sure that Josephina was the suitable bride for him. However, there were two obstacles. First, he had to tell Lord Barrington and Josephina about the duel. Perhaps they already knew and did not care. But it would be ungentlemanly to proceed without being sure. Second, he needed to ascertain if Josephina felt the same way about him, or still did, after she found out. Should both father and daughter be open to his suit, their courtship could begin.

Frederick was on tenterhooks about the dinner, weary that his mother would do something to sabotage his efforts. When the guests first arrived, his mother was standoffish and cold. Pressing next to her, he whispered that she should have a care. She thawed considerably after that. It was not the pleasant, relaxed evening they had enjoyed at Eden-more Abbey, Lord Barrington's home. Though his mother held her tongue, she was not overly engaging. It was Arabella who apologised profusely for her mother's attitude as the guests were leaving.

Once again, Josephina had seen a side to her father she did not know existed. He was a different person when her mother was not present. To her surprise, the distant man had become a person she liked and whose company she enjoyed. On the way home, she even dared to suggest that he take her and Jackson to lunch the following day and was surprised and delighted when he readily agreed.

Then, with a twinkle in his eye, he added, "Perhaps the day after tomorrow would better suit. I thought you would want to attend the hunt tomorrow." And he turned to look at his daughter.

Her eyes flew open wide, and a look of terror came into them. He patted her hand and told her he'd always known. She relaxed visibly and thanked him for the invitation. With her father's blessing, it would not matter that Arabella could not join her. He then suggested that she take Jackson along to save him from having to take the lad. Jackson would be overjoyed! They agreed to have lunch the day after, and Josephina went to bed happier than she had ever been.

The next day, she came face to face with Arabella and Frederick. There was no time to talk as the hunt began. Josephina asked John to watch Jackson, who was so excited she feared he might get into trouble. Still, once the hunt started to move off, his excitement turned to nerves, and that calmed him down.

As the morning passed, Frederick stayed near the ladies, chatting with whoever was closest. Josephina wondered if Frederick was so solicitous with her because he felt as responsible for her as he did his sister, or *does he genuinely care for me*. She hoped it was the latter. She enjoyed his company almost as much as she enjoyed looking upon him.

No disasters befell Jackson, thanks mainly to John, who was well versed in keeping young persons out of trouble. Frederick promised he would bring Henry along on the next hunt. John suggested that they also bring his nephew to watch over the lad. At his suggestion, Arabella giggled.

When Arabella and Frederick got home, they found the house in total upheaval with servants running around and their mother shouting. The reason soon became evident when Prunella burst into the room and flung her arms around Frederick.

It was some time before Arabella and Frederick were able to walk around the gardens with Prunella, and she explained why she had returned earlier than expected. She and George were expecting their first child, and George had sent her home immediately. He wanted her to see proper doctors, and he would be joining her as soon as he could. She said she would stay with their mother for a day or two until her servants got her own house ready, but the Earl suggested she stay as long as she pleased.

Arabella could feel that Prunella was no longer the judgemental woman she had once been. When asked what the latest gossip was, Arabella blurted out that she thought Frederick and Josephina had spent time together and might make an excellent match.

When Prunella raised her eyebrows at her brother, he coloured slightly. Prunella knew all about Josephina's reputation and immediately realised that her mother would do everything in her power to stop such an alliance. For that reason, she agreed to stay. Her brother had suffered enough at their mother's hands, and he had sacrificed it all for her, so she was glad to pay back a little of that consideration.

Prunella had met the redoubtable Josephina many times, as she was her sister's best friend. And she agreed with Arabella that the pair would suit admirably. Neither cared a fig for silly rules and regulations, but both were good, decent people. Yes, she would help Arabella get them together. But first, she wanted to make sure the girl wasn't after a title.

Prunella suggested that they invite Arabella to tea in a few days. During this meeting, Prunella established that Josephina seemed to care for Frederick very much. Satisfied that the girl was worthy, her duty was to inform the girl about the scandal.

"I know all about the duel. It is all in the past, as far as I'm concerned," Josephina replied calmly.

"Certain members of society will cut you dead if you marry my brother. You need to realise that," Prunella insisted.

"Those are the same people that already shun me, so it makes little odds. Besides, I care not for society, and only a few people are of interest to me, and they will not mind. However, Frederick has yet to make his intentions known..." she trailed.

It was a good thing she had arrived when she did. Left to their own devices, Frederick and Josephina may never begin their courtship. Prunella set about acquiring vouchers for Almack's, intending to take Josephina and Arabella and have Frederick accompany them. She firmly believed there was nothing like dancing together to help a relationship along.

Lady Jersey was the only one of Almack's patronesses who approved of Josephina, so Prunella spoke to her. The redoubtable Lady was happy to help and felt such a good match should be encouraged. She pointed out something no one else had noticed but which, once seen, appeared obvious.

"Both Josephina and Frederick had their reputations ruined by their mothers. Had Lady Barrington said nothing, Josephina's behaviour would have seemed only a trifle excessive. Still, the more she expressed public disapproval of her daughter's actions, the more society frowned upon them. As for Fredrick, had he stayed, the whole episode would have been forgotten in a week."

This was another thing Frederick and Josephina shared. It would help each understand the other better and allow them to tolerate whatever rebuffs might come, especially from the two senior women in their families.

Countess Sunningdale thoroughly disapproved of this plan. She insisted that it would somehow affect Arabella's chances.

"If you like, you may chaperone Arabella, and I will chaperone Miss Barrington. We need not spend the evening joined at the hip," suggested Prunella.

Lady Allington knew she was overruled as soon as Frederick reminded her that her days as Countess Sunningdale were numbered. As soon as he married, she would be the Dowager Countess.

Frederick asked for Prunella's advice about the Dower house. It needed some light sprucing up, and he wondered if he should see to the renovations or let his mother manage them to her liking. On the one hand, letting her decorate would give her something to look forward to.

On the other, if she knew she was being removed regardless, he would not be able to threaten her into submission. Prunella agreed it was better to say nothing until it the house was ready.

"Let me do it up. That way, I can say it is a project to keep me busy, and truth to tell, I would enjoy doing it," his sister said.

"By all means," Frederick agreed, "and spare no expense. She is our mother, so make it nice." Then a thought struck him, "You are aware that no matter what you do, she will complain and say she hates it?"

"Of course I am, but I no longer need to care. But Fredrick, I do think you might think about Arabella and Henry. They won't enjoy living so far away from either of us."

"Do not worry. I intend for them to stay with me, even after I marry. They both adore Josephina, and she has grown quite fond of Henry."

"Frederick, have you made your intentions known to Josephina? If you have, she does not seem aware of them," she said.

"Leave that with me. I have a plan," he said.

CHAPTER 6
Awkward Proposal

The assembly at Almack's was a success, with Frederick standing up with Josephina two times. He would have asked her again, but his sisters stopped him. Two dances left open possibilities; three caused a scandal, Prunella explained. He was visibly put out, but she suggested he take her into supper.

Josephina's dance card was quite full. Both the Duke of Barclay and Captain Billings danced with her once, though she refused to dance a second time with either of them. It was Frederick who had the most difficulty finding dance partners. Many mothers had instructed their daughters to refuse him if he invited them to dance. Once he figured out what was happening, he considered himself the luckiest gentleman. He played cards for the remainder of the evening.

Then, an unfortunate incident brought things to a head in a manner both parties would have preferred not to happen. That same evening, Anthony Barlow had also made his first appearance at Almack's since the duel. As the room was packed to the gills, the men had not encountered one another for some time. Frederick had just risen from a card table when he heard a familiar voice declaring, loudly, that he was about to claim a dance from the illustrious Miss Barrington. A hush came over the room as the men clapped eyes on each other. Anthony smiled like the devil himself and left the card room to claim his dance. Frederick followed him out but could do nothing to stop his paramour from dancing with the man.

When the music stopped, Barlow escorted Josephina to the refreshment table. Prunella hastened over and, standing behind Anthony, gestured towards him as she made eyes at Josephina. When Barlow asked for a second dance, Josephina declined. When the man insisted, she said, rather loudly, "Mr. Barlow, I had not realised you were the sort of man who would take advantage of a young lady,"

The gentleman looked confused until Prunella came to stand next to Josephina, a hand protectively around her.

The crisis had been averted, but Frederick knew he had to act soon, lest a worthier suitor take an interest in the object of his affection.

He could not find the opportunity in public to talk to his beloved, but he was determined to express his feelings in the carriage on the way home. He would have preferred being alone with her, but he would have to ignore his sisters and press on.

Frederick turned to Josephina and took her hand in his.

"Josephina, I need to talk to your father tomorrow, but first, I need to talk to you," Frederick started.

"The answer is yes," she said.

Prunella and Arabella, pretending to be deep in discussion, laughed out loud. Frederick glared at them, and they immediately stopped and looked away.

"You must give me leave to say what I have to," he rebuked her.

With a twinkle in her eyes, Josephina replied in a very subtle tone, "I apologise, my Lord. Carry on," and looked at him in silence and expectation.

Thus encouraged, Frederick said, "You know I am no longer considered eligible because of the duel. Do you know that society may not want anything to do with my wife, whoever she is? You must be aware of that before you agree to anything."

"Surely, you must be aware that there is some scandal attached to me, which will affect you as well. And there will probably be more to come. I don't care about money or titles. But I cannot live without horses or rides in the park at break-neck speed. I shall hunt until I cannot seat horse. These are not things that society will like, and this will reflect on my husband, so whoever wishes to marry me must accept this."

Frederick smiled.

"There is one more thing," Josephina added, "I believe my father is unaware that you fought a duel, and I think it only fair to inform him."

"That is what I meant to talk to your father about. What if he refuses?"

The Earl looked stricken.

"Then we shall elope." Josephina looked defiant, but she also looked sad at this prospect.

At this, Prunella cleared her throat.

"I apologise for interrupting. But I would like to point out that, though there has been a reply, there has still not been a proper proposal." Arabella giggled.

"Quite right," replied Frederick.

"Josephina Barrington, will you marry me?" he asked.

"Yes!" she replied and threw her arms around him. He held her as if he would never let her go, and she, feeling so safe and loved, held him too.

Eventually, they broke apart, conscious that they had an audience. Their hands remained clasped together as Prunella and Arabella congratulated them.

CHAPTER 7

Gretna Green

Lord Barrington had been aware of the duel, but he had not been aware of why it had taken place. Upon hearing the tale, he took an immediate dislike to the young Barlow. He commended the Earl on preserving his sister's honour.

He was delighted to give his consent to the marriage, providing it made his daughter happy. His daughter, who had been listening at the door in an undignified manner, rushed in saying she was, and so the three of them sat down to toast the marriage.

Lord Barrington had to end the joyous occasion by pointing out a few facts: Josephina's mother would disapprove and be unpleasant about the engagement.

Josephina informed both men she was not worried about her mother.

"I will tell her that if she opposes the wedding, we will run away to Gretna Green. She knows full well there is only one reason for a hasty elopement and will not risk the shame it may bring on the family. Either way, I will marry him, Papa," she beamed.

"I know you will, and I am glad for you both. And I will be there, even if I must drive to Gretna Green," he added.

Frederick thought the solution would placate his own mother and explained Josephina would not have to suffer his mother's presence in the house after the wedding.

"Poor Arabella and Henry. You cannot mean for them to live with her in the Dower house? They must stay with us," Josephina said.

"I'm glad you suggested it, as that was my hope," he replied.

～

Both matrons were forced to accept the union and made the best of the situation. They had never been properly introduced and soon became fast friends. It was a small ceremony, attended only by close family members.

Though the announcement of their engagement had caused a stir, it died down quickly, and the couple was happy to be forgotten. As predicted, they were snubbed by many after the wedding. They did not care in the least. It was, after all, their honeymoon.

However, as the Earl and new Countess of Sunningdale would be a powerful couple indeed, alienating themselves did not seem prudent. The newlyweds were showered with more invitations than they cared to accept.

"Perhaps I should do something truly scandalous; people would stop inviting us," she suggested to her husband one day.

"I have no doubt you will, but I would prefer if it were accidental rather than intentional," Frederick replied with a smile.

As they set off for a drive, each in their own phaeton. Frederick hoped he would win the race. His wife had an unerring eye for a fast horse and could get the most out of them. The odds were against him. He looked over at his new bride. She was dishevelled and bellowing in a most unbecoming manner as she urged the horse on. He had never thought her more beautiful.

The End

Presenting The Lady

THE LADY SERIES BOOK TWO

CHAPTER 1

The Devil's Scrape

"Oh, Arabella, you simply cannot. A scrape like that is just too much," Josephina said, shocked and worried.

"I have to do something, and I am sure I can think of nothing else," Arabella replied in a tone that dared her friend and new sister-in-law to add more.

"I want to be a part of it. It sounds like a good romp," added a small voice from behind the drawing-room door, as it slowly opened wider.

"Jackson, you should be in bed," admonished his sister.

"I heard Arabella's horse arrive and wanted to see her," the boy said as if that justified anything. His favourite weekends were spent at his sister and brother-in-law's Estate.

"Well, I do not know what Frederick will say about this," Josephina said on a sigh. She wished her friend was less prone to dramatics.

"You cannot tell him. If he knew...."

"If I knew what, dearest sister?" The Earl of Sunningdale strode purposefully into the room. His countenance was more amused than angry.

Josephina enlightened him to his sister's latest idea. At least the part she knew, for her friend had yet to divulge what form this scandal would take.

"She believes if she raises the devil of a scandal, your mother will send her to live with us to wash her hands of it."

"Hogwash. Even you cannot be such a goose," scoffed the Earl, turning to look at the said goose.

"It is not hogwash, and I am not a goose. I am kept prisoner in the house." Her brother raised his eyebrows at this.

"It is true. I must stay in the same room as Mama all day, and she will not allow me to ride unless she goes with me."

"But Mama does not ride."

"Precisely."

"If this is true, something must be done." Frederick was worried, for he could think of no incentive to persuade their mother to let him become guardian to his siblings. He and Josephina had attempted it many times since their marriage. The Dowager Countess was worried about Society's reaction if she sent her children away. She disapproved of her son marrying 'that chit', as she referred to his new wife. He had forced her hand on the issue, and his mother would not let them forget it. She was convinced that Josephina would encourage Arabella to ignore the rules of the Ton. If she only knew that Arabella came up with the most devious schemes, and it was Josephina that had been the voice of reason.

"Dash it all, sister, you cannot. It just simply will not do," stated the Earl.

"Oh, I think it will do excessively well," replied Arabella, tartly

"You cannot ride roughshod over everyone just because it suits you," her brother admonished.

"Henry and I cannot stomach living with Mama a minute longer. And you know very well she refuses to allow us to live with you and Josephina. This way, she will have no choice."

Josephina interjected, "I fear you sadly misjudge your Mama. This will only make matters worse. Now, go home before you are missed. Tomorrow, I will call on the Dowager Countess. If what you say is true and not one of your exaggerations, I will endeavour to set things right."

Before Arabella could reply, the Countess continued. "I am not throwing a rub in the way, as you might at first perceive, but I intend to hatch a Canterbury Tale for your mother. I believe it may work." Then, to her husband, she said, "provided the Earl has no objections."

"The Earl does," he said with a smile. "Why am I not to be included in these Canterbury Tales? Am I not deserving of a little diversion?"

"No. I mean, yes. Oh, dear... Truth be told, I did not want to involve you in deceiving your mother."

"You know I care not a fig for my mother. In fact, I think we shall go in our phaetons."

"Oh Frederick, she will have apoplexy before we even enter the house. You know she cannot abide me driving that sort of gig."

"Good, then we shall have the advantage. Now, sister dear, go home as Josephina says, and she will tell me what she means to do. And you, Jackson, can stop pretending to be invisible and go to bed. Is your sister Sophia with you?"

"She is a girl and is sleeping," the lad replied, as if that explained all.

"Oh, I see," said Frederick, trying not to laugh, "well, off to bed anyway."

Josephina's siblings adored the Earl and obeyed him to the letter, a feat Josephina had yet to master.

CHAPTER 2

The Dowager Countess

O nce everyone had left the room, the Earl sat with his wife and sweetly demanded to know what she intended to do.

When they were married, she and Frederick had hoped to persuade his mother to let his siblings live with them. His mother was a terrible harridan, full of rules and regulations only she saw sense in, and oft-times only she was aware of. Any deviation from these was severely punished. Imagined slights, too, had to be paid for.

She appeared to have devoted her life to making those around her suffer as much as possible. She had not wanted children, nor did she now. But it was her duty to see them through to adulthood. However, she was susceptible to what Society said, so sending her children away was something she could not countenance. It would cause gossip, which was akin to social death.

Josephina intended to use these notions against her.

She planned to tell the Dowager Countess that Arabella intended to do something that would cause a massive scandal. One that would neither be forgotten nor forgiven by the Ton. She and the Earl would be away, staying with the Duke and Duchess of Middlesex, so they could in no way be held responsible. Full accountability would lie with the Dowager Countess. Part of this plan involved a letter Arabella had already given to someone, so the matter could not be halted by confining Arabella in her rooms.

If the Dowager Countess could be imposed upon to send Arabella to advise the new Countess on the running of the Estate, the Ton would see that as a selfless gesture. Naturally, Henry would accompany his sister to ensure her safety. Josephina and Frederick would lend credence to this gammon. It would be believed, Josephina was sure, for such measures were not uncommon.

Since it would be a struggle to keep Arabella from doing anything too rash, Josephina decided now was a good time to let Frederick know some of the larks his sister had tried to cut up.

She recounted when Arabella had presented herself for hunting dressed in a man's garb and ridden astride. Josephina had refused to go with her; Arabella would have continued alone had not her friend been able to sway her from the pursuit. She pointed out that her horses would be confiscated if her mother ever found out; she would never hunt again. Accepting defeat, Arabella had changed into a suitable Lady's riding habit.

The Earl was shocked, for rarely had a worse scandal happened in his memory. He was now unsure about the wisdom of becoming guardian to such a sister. Should she do anything like that again while under his roof, he and Josephina would feel the brunt. His beloved suggested they have a stern talk with Arabella. Should she incite even mildly dishonourable gossip, they would send her back to her mother and never allow her to live with them again. She also suggested that Prunella, as Arabella's older sister, be included in the charade. She may have an inkling of how to control the hoyden.

Once at the Dower House, Frederick informed his beloved that he wished to speak to his sister before talking to his mother. "She must give me her word that she has no actual intention of causing a scandal. Otherwise, I will let her stay with Mama and be done with her."

The Countess saw no point in explaining that what was a scandal to him was merely a lark to his sister. In her innocence, she meant no actual harm.

What neither of the pair had considered was the girl in question's unfailing loyalty to her friends and family. Josephina was as dear to her as anyone in the world, and Arabella would studiously avoid anything that might hurt her friend, if she perceived such damage possible. Should Frederick become her guardian, everything she did would reflect on Josephina as well as her brother.

Frederick contrived to talk to his sister alone by simply expressing the desire to do so.

He informed her that if she were to live with them, there would be no raising a breeze of any kind. She would be the sole of decorum and comportment, he insisted.

"Naturally, brother dear, and if you allow me to hunt, I am sure I shall feel no need," Arabella re-joined demurely.

"Arabella, I will make no deals with you over this. I will not allow you to cause Josephina any problems or embarrassment."

Arabella assured him she would do nothing to harm Josephina, and when he asked for her word, she willingly gave it.

She made a silent vow to improve her behaviour. She would endeavour not to kick up too many larks. In fact, she would try not to do anything untoward at all if that was not too boring. If only they would let her hunt and drive the gigs, she felt sure she would not feel a need.

Frederick returned to the hall and prepared to enter battle against the Dowager Countess. He was happy to have settled the matter, though he was oblivious to the danger ahead.

The Lady was already in ill-humour, for she had been forced to suffer Josephina's presence while her son was talking to Arabella.

Josephina had wanted to be a party to the discussion with Arabella. Still, Frederick had put his foot down and forbidden this. Not knowing what had happened severely hindered Josephina's ability to negotiate a good deal, so she left most of the talking to the Earl. This was something that astonished everyone who knew her. It happened so rarely.

The Earl got straight to the point, wishing to quit his mother's company as quickly as possible. He explained, without going into detail, that Arabella was about to cause a terrible scandal. When asked to elaborate on this, the Earl refused. He would not discuss such matters in front of his mother. This reluctance on his part worried the Dowager

Countess more than anything he could have said, just as he had known it would. And indeed, that had been his intention.

What followed was a long and unpleasant discussion. The Dowager, at first, categorically refused that her remaining children be removed to Sunningdale Manor. When her son and 'the chit' rose and walked to the door, she realised she had lost. Should the Dowager refuse their offer, she would be finished in Society. Believing herself to be an extremely reasonable person, she saw that the arrangement was to her benefit. Society would see she was seeing to the betterment of her beloved children. The fact that it made her new daughter-in-law seem incompetent was an added incentive. It was an excellent scheme. She would be free to do as she wished, but she had conditions.

"Sit down, Frederick. I haven't finished," she ordered.

"Mama, this is not open for discussion. It is a yes or a no." replied the Earl.

"As you've not received a reply yet, perhaps you'll do me the courtesy to sit down and let me deliver it," the Dowager chastised.

Frederick looked at Josephina and nodded imperceptibly. They both returned to the uncomfortable high-back chairs provided for visitors.

The Dowager then proceeded to lay out her terms but was brusquely interrupted, "Let me be clear, Mama,"

The Earl knew from experience that the only way to handle his mother was with an ultimatum, not an offer.

"When I said your answer must be yes, or no, I meant exactly that. You will have no terms, and there will be no negotiation." When that redoubtable woman would have interrupted, he held up his hand to stop her. "If you do not reply instantly, we will take that as a no and go home to pack for our stay with the Duke and Duchess of Middlesex. After all, we do not wish to be associated with such goings-on. We intend to distance ourselves as much as possible.

Josephina was afraid that both parties would be too stubborn to reach an agreement. So, for the first time, she joined the discussion.

"Your grace," Josephina still addressed Frederick's mother using that form, even though they were now peers. The elderly Lady came to expect it. Josephina thought acquiescing was better than dealing with the endless complaints.

41

"The Ton will look on you favourably if you send Arabella to help me. You have my word that no one will ever know the truth of the matter. I do not believe you want a scandal, but I know Arabella. She is capable of doing things that would cause you to swoon at the mere mention of them."

"I can attest to the verity of that statement," interjected her Earl.

Ignoring him, Josephina continued, "Think of the exertion and expense you will save yourself by agreeing to Frederick's guardianship. Should Arabella come out while she is living with us, it will naturally be our responsibility."

Josephina well knew that amongst the Dowager's many faults was her 'purse-pinching'. She avowed that her son continually kept her short, when in reality, she simply was mean and terribly inept at keeping account of her spending. "We shall pay for her gowns, host a ball at Sunningdale Manor, and make all the arrangements, but we will not take the credit. You will present your daughter at court, and the Ton will believe you are bringing her out, not us. That gives you all the benefits without any of the worries."

The Dowager Countess thought this an excellent idea, and it helped make up her mind.

"I could not possibly present my daughter with the toilette I have. My attire is not suitable for court. I should need a new wardrobe, including reticules, hats, gloves. Everything."

A small smile struggled to escape the Earl's lips. Still, getting it under control, he simply said, "That is obviously part of bringing Arabella out, Mama. You must look the part to present her at court."

"Perhaps some new jewels?" the Lady mused out loud.

When Frederick would have admonished her, refusing this request, Josephina said, "We can sort out details at a later time. I am afraid we have an appointment and must take our leave." She shook her head at Frederick, urging him to say nothing.

"Very well," and before the elderly Lady could say more, a loud whoop was heard from the other side of the door. Arabella and Henry charged in and hugged Josephina and Frederick before dropping a curtsy and bow to their mother.

"I would be grateful if you would get their maids to pack them up," said Josephina. She was keen to remove them from the harridan's lair before she changed her mind.

"We have done it. We are ready to leave now," said Arabella and Henry, almost in unison.

"Well, you cannot leave now because we came in our phaetons and there is no room. I will send the carriage for you tomorrow," Frederick stated in as stern a voice as he could manage. He neglected to say that they had raced there, and his beautiful Countess had won, as usual. He believed that knowledge would be too much for his mother, who was already scandalised by Josephina driving a phaeton.

Feeling that she needed to win at least one battle, the old Lady reprimanded her son, "You should not encourage your wife to drive such a carriage. It is most unbecoming and reflects poorly on you."

"Not as poorly as if she were to do it behind my back." He gave his mother a look that left her no doubt that she needed to be quiet on the subject.

She badly wanted to lecture her son on the intricacies of a man who could not control his wife, but seeing his expression, wisely, she stayed silent.

His sister had every intention of getting away that very day. "But we could...."

"Arabella, I said tomorrow." He said more sternly than he had intended.

"Yes, Frederick. Of course," replied Arabella demurely.

No one had ever seen Arabella so agreeable. It almost worried her brother, but he put it aside, believing and hoping it was simply the joy of being set free.

CHAPTER 3

Well Laid Plans

The following day, Josephina had the maids prepare rooms for Arabella, Henry, and their entourage. Arabella had a lady's maid, Henry had a tutor and a governess. The Dowager had also sent a footman along to see to their luggage.

When asked for her input, Prunella had suggested they hire a companion for Arabella. Her school friend, Constance Wellington, was a Lady. However, she had fallen on hard times when her father had lost everything to cover gambling debts. She is now forced to seek employment as a paid companion. She would do a splendid job of keeping Arabella out of trouble.

Constance had come out with Prunella, and they had been presented at court together. She had even accepted the Duke of Wesley's offer. But as her father had become destitute, the contract was cancelled.

Constance loved horses and sat a horse very well. As she also had an interest in hunting, Arabella would have an excellent chaperone for any outing.

Prunella had sent for Constance. When the Earl and Countess returned from visiting the Dowager, the ladies were in the parlour having tea. Frederick and Josephina were much taken with her.

When informed that Arabella had once worn britches and ridden astride, Constance had assured the Earl and Countess that such behaviour would be curtailed.

"Hopefully, Arabella will see you as a friend and companion and not her chatelaine. Even though you would be her 'keeper' as such, you would dine with us, naturally. When we have company, you will be introduced as a friend. I will get my dressmaker to sort something out. As you arrived with only a carpetbag, I can't imagine you've brought many ball gowns."

Constance was so grateful to have found dignified employment. She would have agreed to anything. The fact that this family seemed well-disposed to include here was a benefit she had not anticipated.

The house was put into upheaval the day their guests arrived. Everyone was running about, trying to organise the numerous bags and boxes Arabella appeared to have. Both Arabella and Henry seemed to be in such high spirits that they added to the melee by ordering the servants.

Frederick was tempted to escape the chaos and visit his club. Still, he felt he could not abandon Josephina, so he called his siblings into his study. The Earl gave them a severe dressing down. He reminded them this was no longer their home. It belonged to Josephina, and they could not give orders to the servants. They could make requests or speak to the Lady of the house if they needed something.

When they both demanded their old rooms again, Frederick held firm and informed them they would be occupying the East Wing and not their old rooms. He wished to live with his wife without them constantly underfoot, so they would have a wing to themselves. In contrast, Frederick and Josephina lived in the central part of the house.

When they would have protested, he stopped them. Using the same tactic he used with his mother, he exclaimed, "This is not a negotiation. That is how it will be. If you do not like it, you are free to return to your Mama."

This effectively ended all discussion, and they left the room chastened, at least temporarily.

As it was their first night, Henry was allowed to stay up and join the others for dinner. This was a lively affair. Frederick had to constantly inform his siblings that people of their rank did not behave in such a fashion. He kept an eye on Constance, but she behaved exactly as she should.

After the meal, the women retired. Frederick was left alone with his port and cigar. Had Prunella's husband been here, they would have had a stimulating conversation. As it was, he decided that a visit to his club would take his mind off all this talk of ball gowns and petticoats.

When they were alone, he and Josephina retired to his study and had brandy by the fire. She insisted she had no objection to cigar smoke, and they enjoyed many a companionable evening that way.

As Josephina sat with Arabella and Constance, she missed Frederick and their evenings together. During the day, he had business to attend to, and evenings were often the only time they had to discuss.

"Ladies, would you mind terribly if I joined my husband and left you to get better acquainted?" Josephina had said earlier, after dinner.

Arabella frowned. She had only just arrived and hoped to spend time with her best friend as well as her brother. But Constance only smiled.

When Arabella made to speak, Constance quickly replied, "You are still newlyweds. I understand perfectly. Enjoy the remainder of your evening, my Lady."

"Thank you both for understanding. If there had been male guests, I would not have broken decorum, of course. But this is truly the only time my husband and I have to ourselves. There is much to discuss," replied Josephina, already at the door. "Good evening, ladies," she said and left the sitting room.

"But Josephina..." exclaimed Arabella to Josephina's back.

"Arabella, it is most unbecoming call out in such a manner. Do you not see that Josephina has sacrificed her private life with your brother so that you may live here? Do you wish to be sent back to your mother's?" asked Constance.

Arabella opened her mouth for a retort, but then she suddenly realised Constance was right.

"Oh, Miss Wellington. You are correct. I am a selfish brat."

Constance patted her knee and said, "You may call me Constance as I'm sure we're going to be great friends."

"Yes, I would like that. On another matter, do you have a riding habit for the hunt tomorrow? If you do not, you may wear one of Josephina's. She has many, and you are about the same size,"

"I could not wear the Countess' riding habit!" exclaimed Constance in apparent horror.

"Do not worry. It was Josephina's suggestion as there was no time to have one made for you," replied Arabella.

Constance eyed her with suspicion.

"Come, we shall stop by the study to receive a confirmation on our way to Josephina's rooms."

Meanwhile, when Josephina joined her husband in his study, Frederick was overjoyed, and any thoughts of going to his club had vanished. All the married men at the club had clearly not made love matches if they could bear to be away from their wives every night. Frederick would never admit it publicly, but he understood the meaning of the term Marital Bliss.

His joy faded when their discussion was interrupted by a knock at the door. It was Arabella and Constance, and they stayed but a moment and were gone. Once they had, he locked the door and gave his lovely wife a lecherous look that put her in a fit of giggles.

Once they had obtained permission and received instructions on which habits could be borrowed, the ladies headed for Constance's rooms, where the habits would be brought by Josephina's maid.

The maid offered to stay and assist them, but Arabella assured her they would be fine. If anything more was required, she would ask Lily, her own maid.

The maid left with a curtsy, and the ladies managed well enough on their own. Riding habits were not intricate garments to put on or remove. By design, they were made to be comfortable. At least, Josephina's were fashioned that way.

Constance found one that not only fit her but also complimented her colouring. She had wavy chestnut hair and pale blue eyes. The moss-coloured habit, trimmed in navy, made her look regal and very smart.

"How lovely you look, Constance! I believe the habit suits you better than it does Josephina herself!" exclaimed Arabella.

Constance blushed. She was pleased. It had been months since she'd worn anything so fine.

"Thank you, Arabella. You are very kind. Now that the matter of my attire is settled, I believe we should retire. We want to be fresh on the morrow," she replied.

Arabella was disappointed. She would have loved to chat into the night with her new friend.

"Yes, Constance. Though I am enjoying your company, I believe you are right. Good night," said Arabella.

"Good night, Arabella," replied Constance.

CHAPTER 4

On The Hunt

On the day of the hunt, Frederick left early to collect Jackson. Lord Barrington was easily persuaded, as the boy would benefit without any exertion on his part. Lady Barrington, who knew her married daughter would be at the hunt, was not so easily convinced. She was sure the boy would be safe enough and well supervised. But she wasn't all that keen on letting him be associated with a gentleman who let his wife hunt and drive a phaeton. Even if said-wife was her own Josephina.

The ladies set off for the hunt somewhat later, having no deviations to make. Both Josephina and Arabella were pleased to see Constance sit a horse as well as Prunella had foretold. They should have no worries about her.

For her part, Constance was very excited but trying her best not to show it, mindful of her position as an employee. It took little encouragement from Arabella to free her from these self-imposed strictures, and soon she exclaimed over everything. She was, after all, only a few years older than Josephina, who was in turn only a few years older than her dear friend Arabella.

The hunt officials, now accustomed to having ladies in attendance, kept a bottle of Sherry on hand. An additional stirrup cup was fetched for Constance. Frederick and Jackson joined them just before the off.

Jackson made everyone laugh by declaring he would take care of Miss Wellington. Though Lord and Lady Barrington were under the impression that this was his first hunt, Jackson had accompanied his sister on more than one occasion.

It was a good chase, and to Arabella's delight, they didn't catch anything. She could not bear to see animals being harmed. She only hunted because she could gallop across fields and jump walls. This was not something she could do under normal circumstances. She knew this to be true because she had tried it when she was young. She had been severely reprimanded, and she'd been forbidden to ride for an entire month.

Arabella had not been hunting since the wedding. As the Season would soon close, her family did not intervene when she forged ahead. Frederick and Josephina stayed back to keep an eye on Jackson and Constance.

They had to stifle hilarity on many occasions as Jackson told Constance how he was experienced after five hunts in total and made helpful suggestions. Constance, for her part, took these in good stead and simply thanked him for his help. His chest puffed out as he trod alongside her. Clearly, the lad was smitten.

Once, when the hunt stopped to look for a scent, Josephina saw Arabella chatting to a gentleman she didn't know. As he was a stranger to Josephina, it wouldn't do. She had chastised Arabella on more than one occasion about engaging with a gentleman who had not been properly introduced in the absence of a suitable chaperone. If Frederick took notice, there would be the devil to pay.

Just as Josephina steered her mount in the couple's direction, she saw Constance heading their way at a trot. Josephina reined in to see how that lady handled it.

"Sir, I do not believe we have made your acquaintance?" she said, a bit breathlessly as she joined them.

"The Honourable Rupert Feathering," came his reply as he bowed to the new arrival.

"A pleasure, Sir. How are you acquainted with the Lady?" she said, sidling her horse next to Arabella's.

"I am afraid you have the advantage, Miss... as I do not know your name," he replied.

"It is."

"Do not answer that!" Josephina said in a tone that brooked no argument, riding up to join the party. She manoeuvred her mount to Arabella's right so that the girl was flanked on either side.

"I am the Countess of Sunningdale. Would you be so kind as to answer my friend's question? Have we been introduced?" said Josephina with a haughty expression.

"Josephina, he just came over to talk about my horse," Arabella hoping to take the sting out of the obvious set down.

"Sir, I will thank you not to put my ward in such an untenable position again. And do not consider this an introduction. Arabella, come away now. Good day to you, Sir." Josephina wheeled her horse and found Frederick right behind her.

"I am the Earl of Sunningdale, and I second my wife's sentiments, for no man worth his salt would do such a thing to a Lady. Come, my dears," Frederick insisted.

As they rode off, the Honourable Rupert Feathering fumed. To be set down by a peer was insulting enough. But by a woman, and in the company of marriageable ladies could not be born.

The Earl was displeased. On their first outing as Arabella's guardians, he and Josephina seemed to have failed to protect their charge. Resolving to find out how such a thing could happen, he asked his Countess for her account. Josephina assured him that Constance had handled the matter to perfection. The fault lay with the Honourable Rupert Feathering and Arabella.

He summoned the ladies to his study for a complete account of the events.

"He simply commented on my mount and asked her breeding. There is nothing to fuss about, brother dear," explained Arabella, trying to make light of the matter. For, to her, it really wasn't worth mentioning, let alone be the topic of a grand inquisition.

"I see. And who introduced you to this cad? Where did you meet him?" Frederick demanded.

"No one introduced me. The gentleman approached me as I waited for the rest of the hunting party to arrive. He was clearly a respected member of the Ton if he had been permitted to join the hunt," replied Arabella. Her marron eyes stared back angrily at her brother.

Tempers were about to become inflamed. Josephina quickly spoke up. "Dearest Arabella, do not be cross with your brother. You know as well as I that no respectable Lady ever talks to a gentleman without a proper introduction."

Appalled at being spoken to as a child by her dearest friend, Arabella retorted, "Josephina, you sound like my mother!"

Frederick, calmer now, gave a laugh. "Perhaps we should have left you in your mother's care, as you have clearly do not possess the necessary social graces to be out into Society. No *gentleman* with honest intentions would not have approached an unchaperoned Lady. The fact he felt it right to accost you in this fashion shows that he is a bounder. This is something you know, yet you chose to speak with him anyway. You disappoint me, Arabella. Terribly. You abused my trust and have placed our family in an awkward situation. We were not the only ones to observe the scene this morning. Though, I admit, gentlemen are not quite as prone to gossip as the ladies. However, one or two of them are sure to remark on the incident to their wives or sisters. By teatime, you'll be the talk of the town. This will significantly impair your chances at a good match."

Arabella had the good sense to bow her head in shame.

"We had an understanding, did we not?" the Earl asked.

Arabella nodded mutely.

"That is the last time you will hunt while you are under my roof. I am seriously considering sending you back to your mother and postponing your coming out by a year until you have matured," said the Earl.

"Constance, I apologise for the family drama. Would you and Arabella remove to the sitting room while I discuss the matter further with my husband? Inform the butler that we will not be receiving callers today," said Josephina.

Constance rose and took Arabella by the arm, gently steering her out of the room. "Yes, your grace," she said upon leaving.

When Frederick and Josephina were alone, he asked, "What do we do now?"

"Arabella seemed contrite," said the Countess. "Perhaps we should give her another chance."

"Fustian. Even Constance cannot attend her side every second. She knows better but chose to do it anyway," he replied.

"Perhaps she was merely taken in by a handsome rogue," replied Josephina, tongue-in-cheek.

"Did you find him handsome, Josephina?" the Earl looked put out.

She smiled before replying, "Once could say he is handsome, especially to a young lady such as Arabella. Personally, I find him too foppish and rake-like. He has the look and manners of a libertine and that I find repulsive."

Satisfied that his wife only had eyes for him, the Earl pulled her in for a kiss.

Frederick made some enquiries and could find no mention of the man anywhere. He was not a member of any of the usual clubs, and none of his acquaintances knew of him. That was good news only in the sense that no gossip was likely to have been created if he was not a member of the Ton.

However, the Earl was not satisfied. He hired a runner to secure more information. He discovered that the Honourable Rupert Feathering was, in fact, Mr. Rupert Faraway. The man was a distant relation of the Duke of Worthingham. When asked where Farthing could be found, the runners informed him he was a guest at the Duke's townhouse.

Frederick resolved to pay the Duke a visit at his earliest convenience.

CHAPTER 5

Secret Rendezvous

Arabella hated being at odds with Josephina and her brother. Still, she thought everyone was making too much of an innocent conversation. Besides, Rupert was most handsome, and he had singled her out. Surely that meant he was interested in her. Wasn't that the point of coming out into Society? To meet eligible gentlemen and secure an offer. She hadn't secured an offer, but she was sure that she would when they saw each other again. She had no idea how that would happen now that she'd been forbidden to hunt for the remainder of the Season. She would have to be cunning.

The following day, Constance and Arabella went riding. Constance had found it prudent not to broach the issue with her new charge when they had gone to the sitting room. Instead, she had engaged her in conversation about her interests and accomplishments. Arabella had seemed relieved, and they had spent a lovely afternoon together.

Now that their relationship had a stronger foundation, Constance thought she might offer guidance on how to repair her relationship with her family. It was a necessary first step before gently educating Arabella on how to comport herself in Society. Surely, the girl would listen to a friend, even if she did not listen to her mother or brother.

Unfortunately, Constance had barely begun her monologue when a rider came upon them.

When they returned, Constance sought out Josephina before even changing her attire. She wished to inform the Countess that they had again encountered the Honourable Rupert Feathering on their ride. Arabella had feigned surprised at his arrival, but Constance had the feeling the meeting had somehow been pre-arranged. "I sent him away immediately and forbade him to meet us again. I cannot say what Arabella may contrive," she told Josephina, wringing her hands.

"Thank you, Constance. I must speak to Frederick immediately. If we call you into Frederick's study later, please remain silent and follow my lead. I do not know what direction the conversation will take at present; be prepared."

Constance assured her that she would do everything possible to help and would be prepared for anything. Then went to change.

By the time Frederick came home, Josephina had rehearsed the account she would tell him. She explained the meeting, but added they could not let Arabella know that Constance had betrayed her.

As usual, Frederick agreed with his beloved's idea. Even when her ideas seemed far-fetched, they often produced the best outcomes. She had a keen mind. He was grateful to have been blessed with a wife of such superior intellect.

Once the party was assembled in Frederick's study, he casually inquired about his sister's morning.

"Arabella, did you go for a ride today?"

"Yes. As I do every day. Why do you ask?" She had such a defiant look on her face, had there been any doubts, they would have been removed instantly.

"Did you meet anyone?" asked the Earl.

Colour rushed to Arabella's cheeks, but her voice was steady as she replied, "No, no one."

"Really? That is interesting. My sources beg to differ. Someone came to tell me that they had seen you and Constance out riding today. Did you not see them?"

"Em, no, I did not see anyone," replied Arabella, worried now that they had been observed. But by who, she wondered.

"Well, that is not quite right, Arabella. The person who saw you also saw you talking to the Honourable Rupert Feathering. Is that true?" inquired the Earl.

"Well, yes, but we did not talk. We just crossed paths as we were riding," hedged Arabella.

"You've been caught in a lie. Do you expect me to believe that your meeting was entirely by chance? That the man you met yesterday would happen to be riding on the outskirts of your Estate without invitation?" the Earl all but growled.

"You can believe what you wish. You are making too much of this. Rupert is free to ride wherever he likes, and so am I. If we chanced to meet, that is hardly my fault."

"You are quite right. It is my fault. I failed to inform you about what I found out about your paramour. He is not who he says he is. His name is Rupert Faraway. He is a distant cousin to the Duke of Worthingham. Though the Duke assures me the man is not disreputable, nor is he a gentleman. Under the circumstances, Mr. Faraway's behaviour may be excused. As he is not a gentleman, he cannot be expected to behave like one. You, however, are a Lady and are expected to comport yourself as a Lady. As you are under my guardianship, I decide which occupations I deem suitable, whom you may associate with, and where you may go. As of this moment, you are forbidden to ride. I have had your horse removed from the stable in case you felt the need to disobey me. Yet again," he declared.

"But Frederick, you cannot take Misty away from me. She is my horse!" Arabella wailed.

"Actually, dear sister, she is mine to do as I see fit," Frederick replied.

At this, Arabella started to cry. So many emotions were coming over her at once. Fury at being treated like chattel by her brother. Shame for being so taken to task in front of Josephina and Constance. Heartbreak at being led astray by Rupert.

Josephina joined the discussion at that point. "Dearest, you are not the first Lady to be charmed by an interloper," she soothed. "You are young and impressionable. You thought you were in love. I understand. However, I must agree with Frederick. You seem to be entirely oblivious that Mr. Faraway tried to take advantage of you and very nearly ruined you. Arabella, I never thought I would say this, but I think Frederick should send you back to your mother. At least in the country, you wouldn't get yourself into mischief. In the last two days, you have proved that all you care about is yourself and hang the consequences. As far as I am concerned, you shall pay the consequences of your actions. As you are intent on acting like a child, you take your meals with the children and the governess henceforth."

Josephina had one more thing to add, "Oh, and if you think of running away with the rake, be sure that your brother will cut you off, and even your mother will have nothing to do with you. You will not have a feather to fly with. Should Mr. Faraday offer for you, he will not get his hands on our money. Be sure to tell him of that before you leave this house because I am certain he will no longer be interested in you."

Frederick concluded by saying, "I have placed a footman outside your room. He will follow you whenever you leave your rooms and report to me once you are suitably chaperoned by Constance or a family member. All of your mail will be read. Do not think you can pull the wool over my eyes. I will not stand for it. Go to your chambers at once."

Tears were running down Arabella's face, and yet she was still defiant. "You cannot do this to me. I have done nothing wrong."

"By saying that, you are only confirming that you are totally self-serving, interested only in yourself, your wishes, and your desires. You think you are in love. Like most young people, you believe you are the only one in the world to have the feeling. But you are wrong on that count as well. Josephina and I were very much in love. Yet, we managed to follow proper courtship conventions and comport ourselves with decorum," stated Frederick with some finality.

Arabella fled from the room, and Frederick poured them all a large brandy.

"Constance, I apologise for placing you in this position. Will you continue to keep an eye on her and warn us if she intends to do something foolhardy?" Frederick asked.

"Of course I will. You have both been so good and kind to me. I can never repay you. I will do my utmost to keep Arabella away from Mr. Faraday, although I fear it may be impossible. She is smitten."

"Her horse was simply sent to my country estate. I'll have it fetched if her behaviour improves. However, she seems to feel this person is worth risking anything for, and we need to get rid of him before it goes any further."

"If I might make so bold if someone were to start a rumour that he was having a dalliance with another woman, that might help," Constance suggested.

Josephina's smile lit up her whole face. "Constance, you are clever. That is exactly what we will do."

"Oh no, I feel an escapade coming on, and I am sure I will be expected to participate." Frederick looked at Josephina with love and some humour.

"How right you are, my dear."

CHAPTER 6

Word of Mouth

Josephina persuaded Frederick to take her and Constance to
Almack's. The two women set about making their plan work.
Upon arrival, they greeted their hostesses. They stood near the
worst gossip of the Ton and discussed, somewhat loudly, and
allegedly between themselves, the fact that Mr. Faraday was trying to
pass himself off as the Honourable Rupert Feathering. They also had
made up a name for a Lady. They discussed him dangling after her,
including various exploits he supposedly did to try and win her hand.
The fictitious Lady was an American heiress. When her father found
out the gentleman was not really a gentleman, he ended it by blocking
his daughter's trust fund money. They then said how Mr. Faraday had
run away as fast as he could when he learnt that the Lady would have no
funds.

According to them, he was after some American heiress. They took
great delight in regaling them about Faraday's exploits regarding his
courtship of this woman.

The rumours spread like wildfire, and, by the end of the evening,
the Honourable Rupert Feathering was being cut by most people in
attendance. Daughters were ordered to stay away from him, and he soon
became so unpopular that he was forced to leave.

During the carriage ride home, the two ladies told Frederick of their work. Though he found their antics hilarious, he worried that perhaps they were pushing a scoundrel into doing something drastic.

He was somewhat disconcerted to discover that Constance and Josephina were of like mind in these matters. His loving wife was not afraid of doing anything that would get her the results she wanted, provided, of course, no innocent was hurt in the process. The Earl knew Mr. Faraday to be no innocent, so he was happy to think of him getting his comeuppance.

Josephina had accepted an invitation to tea the following day so that Arabella may hear the gossip for herself. She usually avoided such occasions. Her hostess was most agreeable when Josephina said she would bring Arabella and Constance with her.

When Arabella tried to make conversation in the carriage, Josephina said, "Arabella, I am still very cross with you. I would prefer that we ride in silence."

She hoped she wasn't pushing Arabella too much, but the situation was desperate. She was sure that the girl was good and hoped this infatuation would not be so intense that it would go against her good nature. She was hoping Arabella would feel forced to choose between her family and Mr. Faraday by remaining cool. As she had only just met the man, surely family would win out in the end.

Mr. Faraday's scandalous behaviour was the juiciest gossip the Ton had had in some time. The main question that no one could answer was how this person had inserted himself into the Ton in the first place, and who had acquired a voucher for him to attend Almack's? One Lady answered this by saying he had a secret lover, a married Lady of some standing, and she had acquired the voucher for him. Little did they know, this was actually the truth.

Arabella's complexion got paler and paler until, at one point, she excused herself to get some air. Constance went with her outside. Tears poured down her face.

"Do you think it is true, Constance?" she sniffed.

"I do. I saw him at Almack's yesterday and... Yes, I believe it to be true." She could not bring herself to add more, for it did not seem to be necessary.

"But he said I was the most beautiful Lady he had ever seen," cried Arabella.

"I heard him tell two different ladies the very same thing last evening. Arabella, I know you are infatuated, but he is not for you. You are hurting the family who loves you. I can assure you that Mr. Faraday does not. Painful as it is, he is only after your fortune. If you have doubts, tell him Frederick refuses to pay your dowry if he disapproves of the match. I am sure you will never see him again."

The last utterance totally undid Arabella, and she became hysterical. Constance got her into their carriage before anyone could see and sent a footman to tell Josephina that, unfortunately, Arabella was indisposed and needed to return home. Josephina thanked their hostess and made their excuses.

Not a word was spoken on the journey home. The next move had to come from Arabella. When the carriage pulled up in front of the house, Arabella jumped down and ran to her rooms. No one saw her until after dinner. Dinner had been sent on a tray, but the food remained untouched.

Frederick, Josephina, and Constance were sitting in the dining room with port and a cigar. Only Frederick was smoking, naturally, when there was a knock at the door. Arabella came in and ran to her friend, throwing herself onto her breast.

"Forgive me. Forgive me. Oh, sweet Josephina, please forgive me. I thought he loved me."

And at this point, she started to cry again.

"Arabella, stop crying. He is not worth it. There will be many men who tell you they love you. But there are two things you can do to determine whether they are sincere or not. One is to listen to people around you, and the other is to observe their behaviour. No gentleman would accost you the way Mr. Faraday did. If a gentleman was truly interested in you, he would find a way to obtain an introduction. These are things you must look for. Do not listen to the words alone. When you found out Mr. Faraday had lied about his name, do you not think that people who lie about one thing will lie about another? They generally do. There were many signs. You just did not look at them. I know this is your first love, but I hope never to go through another one like this. Now the whole thing is a bag of moonshine, so let us put it behind us," soothed Josephina, relieved that she could end the charade and embrace her dearest friend.

Frederick poured his sister a drop of brandy, and it did help calm her down.

Arabella's horse was returned, the footman resumed his regular duties, and Arabella's mail was no longer censored.

For a while, life went on as usual.

CHAPTER 7

A Lesson Learned

The incident with Mr. Faraday had forced Arabella to grow up. This aspect of her education had been somewhat lacking. The Dowager Countess had kept such a tight rein on her daughter that she had not provided opportunities to learn from the world. Any time Arabella could escape, she did. Still, her antics remained secret, and thus she was never reproached for her behaviour. She knew what was right and what was not in theory, but in practise, she had done what she wanted with no one to tell her otherwise.

Her countenance changed after her first heartbreak. She was still lively and effervescent, but she paid more attention to other people and their needs. She behaved with greater dignity. There were a few minor scrapes, but nothing to cause any harm to anyone, herself included.

She had resumed hunting and helped Jackson and Constance when they were out, always staying close to a family member.

There really was no need for Constance to stay in the household anymore. Still, Frederick and Josephina had become fond of her, and they decided they wanted her to remain. She helped Josephina organise dinners and balls and basically did anything she could to support the family. Constance loved it there and really enjoyed that they included her in their outings. She was always presented as a friend, never an employee, which gave her the same social standing that she had once had. She never took advantage of them. She was always quick to collect a forgotten handkerchief or give up her place in the shade.

Time passed peaceably, and Arabella's coming out was approaching. This caused no small trepidation in everyone's heart, mainly because it meant her mother would be involved.

The Dowager Countess, as expected, made no one's life easy. When her demands became unreasonable, the Earl threatened to reduce her allowance for Arabella's coming out. This brought the formidable Lady under control. She was so bitter about life that nothing was ever going to satisfy her. This was the reason her children seldom visited, and Prunella refused to leave her child in her grandmother's care unless she was also present. It had to be said the grandmother in question had no interest in babies. She only wished to appear to be the perfect grandmother.

Arabella's mother was to stay for the Season. She would be presenting Arabella at court and at the ball in her honour at Sunningdale Manor. She would also have accompanied her daughter to the Season's assemblies and balls. It would be an ordeal for all involved.

When Frederick took guardianship of his sister, he had not properly thought of the consequences. He had given no thought to the fact that he would have to open his London house to the Ton and even less to the notion that he would have to escort his sister and mother to assemblies and balls.

He did enjoy an occasional ball and would happily have attended as many as Josephina wished. Spending endless evenings in the company of his mother would be unbearable. Yet, it had to be done.

The fact that Josephina seemed to be anticipating the Season with great excitement made it worse. He would have liked her to have been as blue devilled as he, but she seemed thrilled by all the happenings because they were not centred around her.

Arabella had grown more beautiful as she matured. She had no great intellect, but she was personable and loved to laugh. This was to her benefit as gentlemen did not usually care for a clever Lady.

Arabella's blonde trusses always behaved perfectly. They were curled into ringlets that sat precisely where they should, and a few tendrils curled around her face in the way every Lady dreamed of. Her figure, though far from perfect, was easily made to appear so. A very tight corset pulled her in where she needed it and pushed her out where she was lacking.

Unless Arabella's behaviour reverted to her former ways, there was every expectation that she would make a fine match in her first Season. She had the looks, she had the breeding, and she had the money. An overbearing mama might hinder an interesting match, but Frederick had that well in hand.

The Dowager was most excited. She knew few other debutants would be presented with quite as much pomp and ceremony as her Arabella, for few were as flush in the pockets as her Frederick.

However, she descended hours before she was expected. After barking orders at the servants, who set them at odds, and criticising Arabella, she had everyone in high dudgeon by the time Frederick came down.

She persisted in criticising everything her daughter did, and that was what prompted the debutante to disappear. Panic ensued as the household searched for Arabella. Josephina eventually found her sobbing near her horse in the stables.

Arabella refused to enter the house while her mother was there, and she even refused to be presented at court.

Josephina knew that if she involved Frederick in this, he would threaten everyone and make matters worse. Arabella needed to feel calm to be presented, but Josephina was at a loss at how to achieve such a feat.

She sought out Constance, and together they worked out the best way to deal with this new problem.

Frederick would have to be convinced to accompany his mother to court early. He would persuade her it was to search for the best place for Arabella to wait. Then Arabella could be prepared and arrive with Josephina, Prunella, and Constance.

Convincing Frederick was the most challenging part, but as soon as they left, Arabella became docile. She was ready quicker than anyone believed possible. If she thought Prunella would present her, and that her mother had gone back home, that was only a minor misunderstanding.

When she arrived, she was so excited to see all the royals and the splendour of everything. She forgot about her spat with her mother, and everything went off well.

At the ball in her honour at Sunningdale, the Dowager Countess caught a chill. Though she was not seriously ill, it was recommended that she stay abed. Prunella assured her mother that she would take her place in presenting Arabella and keep her apprised of all developments.

CHAPTER 8
Happily Ever After

Arabella was titled the *Incomparable* that Season and suitors abounded. Many of them were not what her friends or brother would consider eligible, being somewhat advanced in years. There were also a few military gentlemen dangling after her, but these would not suit her comportment at all. She could never play a captain's wife, for it was sure she would offend the other wives and likely the Colonel's sensibilities. However, amongst the suitors were three whom Frederick, Josephina and Constance all liked. It appeared that Arabella liked them as well, and she seemed to enjoy playing one against the other.

From Arabella's point of view, there was only one she was truly interested in. Viscount Philip Pommeray. He was magnificent. He was a Corinthian who was almost, but not quite, a dandy.

He took such care with his appearance that some did term him a dandy. His attire was not sufficiently scandalous nor exaggerated to fully merit the title.

Tall, dark, good-looking, and invariably well-dressed, he was also blessed with charm and wit. The only drawback to this paragon was that he seemed less interested in Arabella than the other suitors did. He did not call as often, and he had yet to ask for a second dance. That was why she played one against the other.

When two of the three asked the Earl of Sunningdale for his permission to court his sister and for her hand, he allowed them to address themselves to the Lady. Arabella turned them both down, but this was expected. Ladies often refused the first time a gentleman proposed. It did not necessarily mean they would keep refusing.

Josephina spoke to Arabella about her suitors. She wanted to be sure her friend married for love and for no other reason. This was when Arabella admitted she loved Viscount Pommery. He had not offered for her, and Arabella did not know what else she could do to bring him up to snuff.

Once Frederick learnt of this, he took charge. He spoke to the Viscount, saying that two others had offered for his sister, but he hoped the Viscount would as well because he felt more inclined towards his suit than the others. The Viscount admitted that he would like to do so, for he was in love with Arabella. He was convinced that Arabella did not care for him and would not humiliate himself with an unwanted suit. Frederick put him right on that score, and the following day the Viscount appeared at the house to speak to the Earl of Sunningdale.

Josephina and Constance kept Arabella company while the interview took place. Arabella was highly agitated, and when Viscount Pommeray was announced in the drawing-room, the other two women feigned interest in their needlepoint. Constance soon excused herself to attend to unspecified chores, and Josephina went to fetch the maid to serve tea.

It would not be proper to leave them for too long, but it was long enough for them to exchange private words. When Josephina returned, she interrupted an embrace. Arabella wore a happy glow that told her things had been sorted between them. The Viscount had offered for Arabella, and she had accepted. They were to be married.

Unfortunately, when the Dowager Countess heard of this match, she disapproved. She wanted someone with a loftier title higher than a mere Viscount for her daughter. She said she would never consent to the marriage. A bitter battle between Frederick and his mother ensued, in which neither would give up their position.

Prunella solved the issue by publicly announcing the engagement.

There was nothing her mother could do. If she refused to give her permission, she would need to provide a valid reason, and she had none.

Once again, Society's regard would dictate her actions. She reluctantly agreed to the match. Truth be told, her approval was not strictly necessary, but it was important for the Ton.

~

Arabella made an exquisite bride. Henry and Jackson were pageboys, and Sophia was Arabella's only attendant. It was a small family affair on a gorgeous, sunny day.

The Viscount was lovingly warned to keep an eye on his wife, and the pair set off for their new life at Hamilton House.

Frederick and Josephina were more than a little relieved to hand over the hoyden. They were sure she would cut up some lark or other. It was only a matter of time.

The End

Marrying The Lady

THE LADY SERIES BOOK THREE

CHAPTER 1
Home Alone

Under the retreating shade of the flowering lime tree, Constance Wellington found something almost unheard of for a woman of her position: time to sit quietly and watch the clear waters of the small lake glisten in front of her.

A hired companion, such as she, had her hands full and schedule filled most of the time. Arabella had been a full-time job, to say the least. Being the young sister of the Earl of Sunningdale, Arabella had carried quite a full social calendar. But what had begun as Constance's nightmare had shifted, over time, to quite a pleasing arrangement. Arabella had indeed become a dear friend.

Now, though, Constance's future looked uncertain. What was a hired companion to do once her charge was truly well and married? Certainly, Arabella and her new husband, Viscount Philip Pommeray, needed no further companions on their honeymoon. Arabella's older sister, a dear friend of Constance, would have retained her services, but it meant leaving London for Paris. But without a feather of her own to fly with, the idea of travel on the Continent held little appeal. Was it pride that kept her home then? Perhaps. It was those thoughts that kept Constance company, as she watched distant birds mirrored in the calm waters.

Eventually, she forced herself to stand and shook off whatever dirt her wool-gathering had set on her skirts. Refusing the offer extended by Prunella and her husband, Captain George Fitzsimmons, was the right thing to do. Though Constance was grateful for the offer, she couldn't imagine a life away from London. Furthermore, she had grown fond of Josephina, the Countess. The feeling was mutual. When the Earl and Countess insisted she stay with them, she was saved having to invent a reason to decline Prunella's generosity.

With both Frederick and Josephina away in France for a springtime holiday, it fell to Constance to see to the running of the house until their return for the last ball of the Season in late June. That left enough time to watch birds circle the lake and to ensure the sun rose and set as it should.

Not that there weren't plenty of other activities with which to occupy herself. There had been a flurry of activity those first few weeks after Frederick and Josephina's departure. First, she'd seen to Arabella's wedding-related correspondence. The small ceremony had been put together quickly and had included only close friends and family. But there had been several letters and parcels to deal with. As it would be unseemly to reply in a month, the task fell to Constance when Arabella returned from her honeymoon.

In the meantime, other correspondence held Arabella's attention, keeping her mornings quite busy. Due to Arabella's successful launch into Society, Josephina was now the most sought-after Countess. Invitations had started pouring in, and someone had to answer them. Left to her own devices, Josephina would have refused them all. Thankfully, Constance had a more refined sense of what was considered proper and she could guide her new friend in these matters. She had done her best to tactfully explain to the Countess of Sunningdale that her position in Society came with specific duties she could not ignore.

Overwhelmed by her new role, Josephina had finally given over these decisions to Constance with no small measure of relief. She instructed Constance to decide which events she had to attend, relying on her to make the appropriate decisions. Not that she hadn't taken the first opportunity to escape from the endless round of balls and other such social activities. When the chance to travel to France had manifested, she and Frederick pounced on it. Since Henry, the Earl's younger brother, had demonstrated an interest in a career at sea, they brought the lad, along with his tutor and governess.

The plan was for Constance to stay behind to see to household matters at Sunningdale Manor until Arabella came back from her honeymoon. Constance would then join the newlyweds at Hamilton House to assist her new friend in any way necessary.

This meant that Constance was entirely at her leisure until the Viscount and Viscountess Pommeray sent for her.

"Excuse me, Miss Wellington."

Constance looked up from the view of the lake to see Lily, one of the maids, holding a silver tray.

"What's this?" asked Constance frowning in confusion at the proffered folded square of paper which sat alone upon the salvor.

"'Tis a letter, Miss," replied Lily.

"I can see that, Lily, but it seems to be addressed to the Earl of Sunningdale." Constance gave her a sharp look. The Earl's correspondence was no business of hers.

"Yes, Miss. But it's from Lord Allington," said Lily, pushing the tray closer to her mistress.

Constance frowned, trying to place the name. She wasn't altogether sure who Lord Allington was.

"Do you mean Henry?" she asked finally when no other name presented itself.

"No, Miss. I mean Lord William Allington, the Earl of Sunningdale's uncle. The former Earl's brother" explained the maid.

"Then it is clearly personal correspondence. I cannot open it," replied Constance, horrified at the suggestion.

"I understand, Miss, but we haven't heard from Lord Allington since the death of his brother. What if he's been taken ill or is planning to visit? The contents of that letter might be time-sensitive," said the maid. "James, the butler, suggested I bring it to you. If Lord Allington is coming to London, we need to be adequately prepared."

"Oh, yes. I see," said Constance, taking the letter from the tray. "Though I am sure you will be more than up to the task if he is coming. But if he is ill...."

Lilly waited, the tray clasped in her hands behind her back.

Constance bit her lip and took a few seconds to debate whether or not to open her employer's private correspondence. Finally shrugging, she cracked the seal and unfolded the single sheet of paper. She read the short letter and sighed with relief.

"What does it say, Miss?" asked Lily on tenterhooks.

"You and James were right. It appears that Simon, Lord Allington's son, was injured while playing cricket at Eton. As Lord Allington doesn't keep a house in town, he hopes to stay at the family home on his way to fetch the boy. His daughter, Penelope, is joining him and would stay here while he goes on to Eton," explained Constance.

"Does it say when they will arrive?" asked Lily.

"He says to look for them on the 4th of June," replied Constance, after scanning the letter again.

"But that's tomorrow, Miss!" exclaimed Lily.

"Well, then I should say I have had quite enough of lying about! Come, Lily, there is much to do."

CHAPTER 2
Unexpected Guests

S unningdale was more than ready for Lord Allington when he arrived with his daughter after supper on the next day. James and his staff were exemplary in their efforts. If the guests were surprised to find the family away from home, they showed no sign. At least they were easy enough to entertain. As they were travel-weary, a footman showed them to their rooms upon arrival. Constance was told that they had no energy for even the slightest repast and went straight to their beds. She breathed a sigh of relief over how simply the visit was taking care of itself. She gave herself over to a quiet evening, thankful matters were not more complicated.

Of course, this did not mean she that wasn't curious about the strangers within her care. From the staff, Constance had garnered more information on Lord Allington. The man was ten years younger than his brother, John, the previous Earl of Sunningdale. When John inherited the title, William had inherited the lesser title of Baron and an Estate in Suffolk.

Within the year, he had married Lady Elizabeth Winthrop, and the union had produced two children. Simon was eighteen and in his last year at Eton. Penelope was seventeen and not yet out into Society. Lady Elizabeth had died the previous year, and the family was only recently out of mourning.

Under the circumstances, it was unfortunate that none of their relatives had been on hand to greet them. Constance was glad that, at least, she was there to answer their questions on the morrow.

With this in mind, she rose early and ensured that her guests would want for nothing. Breakfast was arranged to please even the most finicky palate. Fresh flowers were arrayed in every room. She even saw to ensuring that suitable mounts would be available if their guests required morning exercise. She would delay her own ride to accompany the young lady, should she wish a turn about the property.

Well satisfied that she had managed matters efficiently, Constance was having tea in the breakfast room when Lord Allington entered with a cheery, "Good morning, Miss Wellington!"

She had been so focused on her musings that she very nearly dropped her cup.

"Good morning, Lord Allington. I trust you slept well?" she replied, eyeing the stranger that stood before her.

"Very well, thank you, Miss Wellington," he replied as a footman served him a cup of tea.

Surely he could not be the same man she had briefly met the night before. The Adonis before her could not be more than forty-five. His wavy mane of auburn hair held but a mere touch of grey at the temples and he was sporting a freshly shaven cheek. His blue eyes twinkled with mischief as he took his place opposite her at the table, eschewing the seat at the head of the table. Even in the Earl's absence, no one dared sit in the place of honour.

They exchanged pleasantries while the man had breakfast. Soon the topic switched over to the absent Earl and his Countess.

"I'm afraid I do not expect them back for at least another fortnight. However, Arabella should be returning from her honeymoon within the week. I am sure she would be delighted to see you and her cousin Penelope," explained Constance.

"Yes, that would be lovely. I am sorry I missed the wedding," said Lord Allington.

"I understand you are only recently out of mourning." She hesitated over her next words, hoping to not cause her guest undue grief. "I am very sorry for your loss, my Lord." She had no idea if Lord Allington had been invited or not to Arabella's, or even to Frederick's, wedding. It stood to reason that, because they had been in mourning, they would not have attended even if they had. Or at least, so she hoped.

"Yes, thank you," he replied, wiping his mouth and setting the napkin on the table as he rose. "I really must be off."

She had said the wrong thing after all then. Lord Allington's face had closed off at the mention of his late wife. That he was leaving only underscored the blunder.

"Are you going for a morning ride?" asked Constance, getting up as well, thinking to somehow rescue the conversation, that they might part at least on good terms.

"Of sorts. I'm off to Eton to fetch my son. I expect I shall be back in a day or two," he said as he strode towards the door.

"But, Lord Allington, what of Penelope?" she asked, her voice rising with a note of panic. Of course, the letter had said she would stay at the estate while he went on alone, but she had had no instruction regarding the girl.

"She shall stay here with you, of course," he replied, frowning as though that should have been obvious.

"But we are not acquainted. Miss Allington is still abed; won't she be very cross to find you gone when she comes down for breakfast?" asked Constance. She was not one of those ladies who fussed and wrung their hands at the slightest hint of difficulty. Still, she had not been properly introduced to the young Miss. It felt wrong somehow to simply leave her here with strangers.

"Were you not hired by the Earl to be Arabella's companion?" he asked, his hand braced on the door jamb.

"Yes, my Lord," she replied, shifting uncomfortably under such an intent look.

"Then you are more than qualified to oversee my daughter for a few days. As we have been travelling in close quarters for days, I trust my daughter will not miss me when she wakes. Furthermore, do not expect the child any time before the noon hour. She'll likely send for tea and a bath upon rising. Your mornings will be quite leisurely, I assure you," he replied.

"I see," replied Constance with a forced smile. It seems the matter had already been arranged. Constance tamped down her annoyance and reactivated her manners. "I had a mount prepared for you; the grooms will see to it," Constance fell back on formalities, finding comfort in propriety.

"Thank you, Miss Wellington. I look forward to getting better acquainted with you upon my return," said Lord Allington with a bow.

"Safe travels," replied Constance to the man's back.

As it was only midmorning, Constance left word with the housekeeper to let her know when Penelope awakened. Though she was now obligated with a new charge, she believed she had plenty of time for a long morning ride. Especially if the young Miss would not rise before noon. Good spirits restored; she stepped outside and waited for her mare to be brought around. The air was getting warmer as summer approached. Soon, it would be warm enough to go boating upon the lake.

Constance loved the water. There had been a small pond on her father's estate where she used to enjoy going boating. She had spent countless summer days there with her governess. Miss Silver had stayed on as a companion until Constance came out into Society. Her mother had died birthing her, and she had no other relatives.

Miss Silver would have likely stayed until Constance's wedding. She had to accept another position when her father's finances ran out. Father went to debtor's prison, and Constance, trying to escape the terrible disgrace of her family's downfall, had moved to London in search of employment.

It had been pure luck that she had crossed paths with Prunella at the modiste. Constance had said that she was looking for a new hat to wear, neglecting to mention it was for her interview at the Agency. She had, in fact, just sold her wedding trousseau.

The rest, as they said, was history. Though Constance's life had veered off-course, she had to admit she was much happier than she might have been as the Duke of Wesley's wife. The man had been an utter bore and considerably older than she. As it was, she was safe and well cared for. She lived in one of the best houses in London, received a generous income, and was starting to hope that she might marry a gentleman someday. Constance was not quite a spinster yet. All in all, things were looking up.

CHAPTER 3
Empty Nest

After her ride, Constance changed into a day dress and went to the sitting room to wait for Penelope. She settled with her book on the window seat. So engrossed was she in her novel, she didn't hear Lily until the maid was upon her.

"Good heavens, Lily. Must you sneak up on me thus?" she asked, placing a hand to her startled heart.

"I'm sorry, Miss. I've come to tell you that luncheon is ready when you are," explained the girl.

"Thank you, Lily. Is Miss Allington still abed? Perhaps we should wake her," said Constance.

"No, Miss. Miss Allington has up and gone," replied Lily.

Constance sat up, the book she'd been reading tumbling to the floor in her haste. "What do you mean gone? Gone where?" asked Constance, her voice going uncommonly shrill.

"I don't know, Miss. All I know is that a carriage came for her while you were out for your morning ride," explained Lily.

Constance shot to her feet. "Why wasn't I told about this?" She paced to the window as though to see the carriage still, though it had been gone for hours now if what Lily said was correct.

"I'm sorry, Miss. I –", stammered Lily.

It wasn't Lily's fault. Constance had only mentioned Penelope to the housekeeper in passing. She should have given more precise instructions regarding the girl. In part, she hadn't because the staff had better things to do than keep tabs on a young visitor, especially with their masters away and only a paid companion in residence. In her defence, it had never occurred to her that the girl would simply leave.

No, the servants weren't to blame. Anyone who had noticed the chit had likely thought she'd gone with Lord Allington. Why would anyone have thought anything amiss?

In the meantime, poor Lily looked as though she might start crying at any moment. "Don't worry, Lily. I'll look into it," she assured the girl, though she scarcely knew where to begin.

"What about luncheon, Miss?" she asked.

Constance had entirely lost her appetite. Besides, she had to locate her lost charge in all due haste.

"I'll send for you when I'm ready to eat," she said, dismissing the girl. "I must speak with James."

The interview with the butler did not yield satisfactory results. All the man could tell her was that a Barouche had come for the Lady. As the top was raised, he did not see who was inside the carriage.

"Is there any way to make inquiries as to the owner of the Barouche?" asked Constance.

"I'm afraid not, Miss," replied the butler.

Constance thanked the butler and headed back to the sitting room. On her way, she stopped mid-stride. Perhaps Penelope had left a note for her father. Constance almost ran to the front hall to examine the mail tray, hoping the day's post had not yet been sent.

She was in luck. To her relief, the tray contained a note addressed to Lord Allington. Constance snatched it quickly before she was observed and carried it back to the sitting room to read.

She sat for a moment with the letter. It was written in a Lady's flowery hand. It stood to reason that Penelope had written it. But what if it wasn't? It was one thing opening the Earl's mail. She was close to her employers, and they would surely understand her motives.

This, though, was another matter entirely. Constance and Lord Allington were barely acquainted. It would be a severe violation of privacy to read a letter from a Lady intended for someone else. But indeed, this was an emergency.

This would be the second time she had violated the sanctity of the letter entrusted to her care. Did she dare interfere again? Did she dare to *not* interfere?

"Dash it all," mumbled Constance as she cracked the seal. She unfolded the letter and verified the signature to ensure Penelope penned it. She sagged into the cushions in relief upon remarking that it had.

The note was brief. In essence, Penelope informed her father that she would be shopping with some friends this afternoon and that Miss Hortense Blakely was sending a carriage for her.

While innocuous, the explanation seemed perfectly reasonable to Constance. With the matter settled, she pocketed the note and called for luncheon to be served in the garden.

After a few hours of reading, Constance felt she needed a bit of exercise. She advised Lily and the butler to fetch her immediately when Miss Allington returned. Constance had her horse saddled for an afternoon ride once, assuring herself that the girl would not slip between her fingers again.

Fresh from her ride, Constance was in great spirits when she came down from her chamber. It was nearly four, and she was eagerly awaiting Miss Penelope's return. She could do with a bit of Society. Though Constance had enjoyed her little holiday, she had to admit she was now quite bored. There was only so much reading, stitching, and riding one could do in a day.

She had numerous acquaintances in London, but she hadn't felt comfortable calling on any of her former friends. Her station had changed, and she had yet to make any suitable friends. Though Prunella, Josephina, and Arabella would surely call her a friend, they were absent at the moment. And they were, at the end of the day, *employers*, and she couldn't allow herself to forget that.

At half-past four, Constance started to worry. At five, she had a footman deliver a message to Miss Blakely.

When he came back with the young Lady's reply, Constance felt ill. Miss Blakely had not received a call from Miss Allington. She hadn't seen the girl in more than three years.

Heart quaking within her breast, Constance quickly penned a message to Lord Allington. He had to be notified at once. She included Penelope's note in the envelope and prayed a messenger could locate him in time. The whole matter had become quite untenable indeed.

CHAPTER 4
Bit Of Muslin

"**M**iss Wellington," he said.

Someone was shaking her awake. No, a man was shaking her. A footman? The butler? How had a man entered her room? She always locked it upon retiring. As her sleepy brain roused, she came to the sudden realization she was not in her chamber after all. She had fallen asleep on the settee.

She blinked a few times and opened her eyes. There stood in front of her the most dashing man she had ever beheld. She smiled dreamily up at him and offered her hand. Lord Allington frowned and assisted her to a sitting position.

The warmth of his hand roused her in a way his words had not. She was fully awake now. A hand flew to her hair. What a fright she must look. Oh, forget the hair; what must he *think* of her to lose his daughter in the way she had?

Constance shook the haze of sleep from her hand and cleared her throat. "Lord Allington, what time is it?" she asked, already fearing the answer. The sun streaming through the windows told her what her protesting muscles had already tried to convey. She'd clearly been asleep upon the settee for quite some time.

"It is morning Miss Wellington," he replied. "Have you been here all night?"

"Yes, I guess I must have," she answered. "I was so distraught, I could not make myself go to bed. Do tell me, has there been any news?"

Maddingly, he did not answer, his silence saying more than words ever could. Lord Allington took a step back and placed his hands behind his back as though waiting for Constance to compose herself, his expression sombre and stern.

Oh, dear.

"Where is your son, my Lord?" she asked, hoping at least that part of his errand had met with success.

"He'll be along later. When the messenger caught up to us, we were having supper in Reading. As he could not ride, I hired a carriage to take him back to London. I left immediately on horseback and only just arrived," he replied,

"My Lord, do you mean to say that you have ridden all night?" she asked.

"Indeed. Wouldn't you if your daughter's welfare was in jeopardy?" he asked a bit frostily.

"Of course. What a dreadful situation," Constance said, thinking how it must have looked, her sleeping when she should have been doing more. Though what this would have entailed, she wasn't exactly sure.

"I fear I must apologize. I should have guessed that Penelope would try something like this," he said with a sigh.

Wait. This was not unexpected behaviour?

"Well, you might have mentioned that!" retorted Constance. Perhaps she wasn't entirely awake after all, given how her tongue seemed to run on without her. "When I came back from my morning ride, I was informed that she was gone. I have not met your daughter, Sir, but she sounds like a handful, Sir!"

She had only just stopped herself from calling the young Lady a bit of muslin to his face. This was neither the time nor the place for such criticism.

Lord Allington took another half step backwards, and for a moment, his face grew as dark as an oncoming storm. Constance feared that she had overstepped her place, or worse, had conveyed, with the look upon her face, what she had almost said. She took a breath, meaning to apologize, but his ire seemed to dissipate with a heavy sigh.

"I suppose that was called for." The admission came reluctantly. "She is...different...since the death of her mother."

There seemed little she could say to this. Constance still felt as though she needed to apologize, though for precisely what she wasn't sure. All she knew was that she had caused, however indirectly, pain to enter that handsome face, and she regretted that. Looking at him now, she wanted to smooth that tortured brow, to ease his sorrow and frustration.

She wondered what he was like under different circumstances. What it would sound like when the man laughed, for example. She imagined it to be a deep, throaty laugh, one that came from the depths of his soul.

"Miss Wellington?"

Constance suppressed a gasp. She knew that he had just asked her a question, but for the life of her, she didn't know what it was. How could she be so distracted by a man's appearance?

"Forgive me, Sir, I was trying to think of where she might have gone. There are few places around here. Perhaps one of the other families came to call and invited her out?"

"Yes..." He looked at her strangely, as though he was reconsidering his opinion of her, and it wasn't going well she thought. *He likely had a point*, and she kicked herself for her wool-gathering mind. "Yes, well, we can get back to that. In the meantime, we work with what we know. Miss Wellington, please summon the entire staff at once. I will address them in the ballroom."

"Yes, Sir." She curtsied and tried to repress a shudder. Of course, he thought her a fool. She'd certainly been acting the part. Why would he not?

CHAPTER 5
Flurry of Footmen

"As many of you already know," Lord Allington spoke loudly and clearly, as though addressing military troops. The maids and footmen and even the redoubtable James seemed to stand straighter somehow, as if responding to the power in the man's voice. "My daughter has been gone for some time. From what I gather, she was seen entering a barouche yesterday. Such conveyances do not spring up from the ground fully formed with a horse in harness. It had to come from somewhere."

He paused, waiting for that to sink in a bit before continuing. "Whoever sent for her had to know my daughter was here, and that she'd been in residence less than a full day. Is there anyone here who might have taken a message from her to a house or family nearby? If so, I ask that person to come forward without the risk of discipline. I only seek to find her and be sure of her safety." He scanned the faces of the gathered staff, but the only answer was silence.

"Very well. Miss Wellington?"

Constance jumped at the mention of her name. She had been standing next to him, as was her place, facing the gathered crowd of servants. "Yes, Lord Allington?"

"I would ask that you pen letters to the nearest houses and ask after my daughter. James," he turned to the butler, "I would ask that you would deplete your staff here and send these missives out to every direction."

He must have heard the quiet gasps from the back as he turned once more and addressed the rearmost staff. "I realize that I invite scandal from the Ton, but my focus is now on finding my daughter. I leave it to her discretion to provide whatever practical reason she has for being away thus, but what matters now is her health and welfare." He turned once more to the butler, "James, you may dismiss your staff."

As the staff filtered out, a few of them gawking at the fine appointments of the ballroom, Constance thought the letters to be superfluous. A young, unescorted Lady from a fine house had gone the night through? Such salaciousness would fly through the Ton faster than any missives could find their way into the hands of gossipers. Even were the Lady kidnapped and spirited away, her reputation and her fortune with Society was in dreadful question.

She stole a glance at Lord Allington, only to be surprised to find him looking right at her. He glanced away as she met his eyes, so she might have been mistaken. Perhaps it was James he was looking at. After all, the butler was standing near her, ushering his people through, and assigning them specific duties as they left.

Allington, though, stood tall and unyielding; a statue created by a master sculptor. Had it not been for the fear in his bearing that seemed to weigh on him, he could have been Apollo in the clothing of the day.

"Miss Wellington."

"Yes, James?" This time, she was not caught out. She responded instead of staring off like a fool when the butler called her. Though the handsome view was more compelling even than the lake had been the previous day.

"I can lend you, Abigail, if you like. She has a passing good hand with letters. Though her choice of words is often questionable, she will produce a fair copy."

"I'm sorry?" Constance tried to figure out what he was saying, but it wasn't connecting.

"For the letters?" James's eyebrow rose significantly.

"Oh, yes. Of course. Thank you, I am sure Abigail would be of immense assistance."

CHAPTER 6
Woman of Letters

L ord Allington tried not to pace. People who paced showed that they were worried. And that they were beyond controlling themselves, let alone others. To find his daughter, he had to repress the naked fear he felt for her safety. There was no other way to organize the efforts required to...

Damn the girl. Why did she have to choose now, here, to run off? At home, he could cover for her, make it known that she was strong-willed. At least there, he could have spared her the thrashing that the Ton would give to her reputation.

There were too many servants, too many tongues wagging in London. The Blakely girl was likely to be the first to spread the rumours. Penelope had lied. He forced the air from his lungs and stared out the window at the lake below him. Perhaps it was already too late to avoid a scandal. Perhaps Penelope's situation was irretrievable, but that had little worry for him. That was for tomorrow. Today must find her; alive, healthy.

He kept his eyes resolutely on the blue waters. But they kept wanting to stray where they should not go. Along the waterside, Miss Wellington was a visual feast. A woman of beauty and grace and, from all accounts, wit. True, she hadn't made a good start of it, but then, neither had he.

His wife had died less than a year ago, but the heat between them had died many years before. She and Penelope had been close, closer than any mother and daughter he'd ever met in Society. They tended to forget the men in their lives. Perhaps had he not doted so on his son. Maybe it was his fault...

He shook off those thoughts. That, too, was a matter for a future day. Today, it only mattered that...

"My Lord?"

He turned to see Miss Wellington standing beside him, a look of concern on her face. How long had he been standing lost in thought? For a moment, he thought her look to be one of pity, and his back rose. But when he looked at her again, she was softer than that. She was concerned for him.

"I just wanted to say how sorry I am." She turned her eyes to the distance as if she couldn't face him directly. "I should have been here. I should have stood sentinel outside the Lady's door...I..."

The notion of Miss Wellington parked outside his daughter's rooms elicited a faint smile upon Lord Allington's face. "Had you stood sentinel outside her door, as you so eloquently put it, she would have only shimmied through the window. You would not have prevented her from leaving. Though I daresay she would not have gotten far, had she suffered a broken bone or two from the inevitable fall."

"I was wondering...." She turned back to him, and he fell into her dark blue eyes. They caught him, bright and clever, anchoring her high cheekbones upon her alabaster face. Her mouth seemed like it was made for smiling. Though there was a long history of trial in her face, it still held the beauty and warmth of a girl. It was easy to imagine what she was like as a child, though she couldn't be too much older than that now.

"...is there anywhere around here she might have spoken about, or some activity she was looking forward to, or an acquaintance who lives in the area?" Constance whispered, feeling suddenly flush.

Lord Allington closed his eyes for a moment, let the pain pass until he could speak. "I have been wracking my mind for just such information, Miss Wellington. I must confess I have not listened as often or as intently as a father should. Penelope had always been Louisa's child more than mine. She had a way with our daughter I never had."

"I understand."

"You do?"

She smiled, though her eyes contained a sweet sadness which belied the action, "I too have a father." Her right hand fluttered between them as if she hadn't decided quite what to do with it, a tiny bird caught between their bodies. "I can imagine...."

He captured her fingers in his and held them briefly to his lips. "Yes, I believe that you can."

He released his thumb, allowing her to withdraw the hand at her leisure, but it remained folded around his. Warmth ran up his arm. Her lips parted, her head tilted, though her eyes widened like an animal trapped in a cage. No, it wasn't fear in her eyes. It was something else entirely. It was something he'd seen but rarely, something for which there were no words. He only had to lean down and press his lips to hers... He didn't remember bending over to her. When had his head been close enough to hers, that he could smell her hair, feel her breath?

"Miss Wellington." James cleared his throat from the door.

The girl tore her arm from his grasp. Strangely enough, his hand seemed colder, emptier than it ever had. She held her hand to her chest as though it had been burned. The heat that lit her face now and threatened to rise from the trunk of his neck. He looked up. James was standing at attention, a maid behind him. They looked on, disapproving.

"Miss Wellington, Abigail is yours for the day. When her duties are discharged, please return her to the upper floors." He bowed perfunctory, "My Lord." He turned and walked away, but Abigail remained, a look of amusement taking the place of the disapproval. For all her apparent friendships, Constance was, after all, a hired companion, not exactly suitable for a widowed Earl.

"Follow me." Constance snapped. The moment between them was clearly past. She walked from the room without a backward glance, her back stiff with embarrassment. He stood, abandoned at the window, but the lake no longer held any interest for him. He turned his head, allowing his gaze to rest on the retreating back of Miss Wellington. She was straight and thin, and yet there was a strength in her movements that fascinated him.

He schooled himself, telling his roving eye he needed to find his daughter, but it wasn't the first time the head-strong girl had run off on some grand excursion. Though this time, she had been gone overlong. Alarmingly so.

Which left only one action for him to do. To wait. Eventually, some clue would come to light, giving him a direction to ride, a place to go where he could find Penelope and carry her home. The inactivity chafed. He was a man more used to action than idleness.

He carried the tension with him to his rooms. He allowed himself to think of holding Constance's hand in his, seeing her bright eyes, her timid smile, and he felt lighter somehow.

It was very much like seeing the sun on a storm-clouded sky. Right now, he needed comfort where he could find it.

CHAPTER 7
Conspiracy of Tradesmen

A s soon as she or Abigail finished a letter, it was whisked away. Breathless valets and footmen immediately dispatched them to anyone who might have sent a carriage for Penelope. Their mail service assembly line implied that families of wealth would be gossiping about the girl before sundown.

Each messenger was instructed to await a reply, should the intended recipient not be in residence. While they waited, they were to glean as much information from the servants there as they could. By the time the last letters were penned and sealed, and the bearers of such letters were sent off, the first responses had returned. There had been no sign of Penelope, nor had anyone heard from her for some time.

Constance flexed her fingers and massaged her palm. Abigail stretched, and Constance could hear the woman's shoulders pop as she set herself to pen some more. Bending over a desk used a different set of muscles than housework, and the woman had stiffened up. The two exchanged sombre glances without speaking, a sisterhood formed of sorrow.

The sitting room looked out over the lawn, but the lake was at the other end of the house. Constance regretted that just now, she could use the waters to soothe her. Writing letter after letter had kept her occupied and taken her mind off of the feeling she had when he bent to kiss her.

He *had* intended to kiss her, yes? She swallowed the idea. They had only just met, after all.

Silly woman. She scolded herself even as she dismissed Abigail with profuse thanks. *Concentrate on the missing girl.* It was no good; she couldn't concentrate. As the hour rolled by since the general meeting, Lord Allington grew more upset the longer the search dragged out. He'd kept to his rooms but apparently wasn't able to remain there. He'd come storming out twice, though he had not lost his temper or made a spectacle of himself. For a man like him, inaction was torturous.

"Miss Wellington." Eleanor, one of the maids, stood in the doorway with a tea service. The tea was still steaming, and it looked as though she had thought to include some of the cook's biscuits and butter. Constance suddenly realized she was hungry, as the aromas played with her and informed her how long it had been since she'd filled her belly.

"Eleanor, you *are* a dear." She smiled at the girl and took the tray from her. "I have been a bit...snappish today; please forgive me."

"You've not been snappish," the girl grinned back, "you've been hungry. 'Tis hard to be...Miss?"

Constance had stopped listening. She was staring at the tray, specifically at the small ewer of milk that sat beside the dainty teacup. "Eleanor..." Constance spoke from a small voice, a part of her mind that wasn't working a puzzle. "Is the milk fresh?"

"Oh, dear!" Eleanor rushed to take the tray back from her, "I am so sorry, Miss...I...."

Constance refused to leave the tray in the girl's hands. "No." She stared at the girl and spoke clearly as though she spoke to a child. "When was the milk delivered?"

"Just this morning, Miss." Eleanor stared at her as if she'd lost her mind. "I was sure it was fresh."

Constance thrust the tray into her hands and pushed past the confused maid. "JAMES!" She yelled the man's name twice, throwing herself down every hallway until the butler appeared next to her, a look of stern disapproval on his face.

"Miss?" She could tell she was making a spectacle of herself, but at this time, it didn't matter in the least.

"The milkman, James. Does anyone know where he lives?"

To give him credit, the butler didn't even blink at the strange request. "Indeed, the cook's assistant has gone there on occasion when we have run low...."

"Send a carriage." Constance interrupted him. "As quickly as a horse can be put into a harness. Bring the man here."

"Miss Wellington, I assure you, if there is an issue with the milk...."

"James." She took a moment and collected herself. "Please?"

The butler hesitated, the conflict playing on his face. He took a breath, and a smile won over his hesitation. The look he gave her was of an indulgent father for a favoured child. "Yes, Miss, I'll have him here in a few minutes. May I ask if this is about the missing girl?"

"It might well be, but I don't wish to say anything yet. The Lord is worried enough. There is no need to worsen his concerns."

James nodded and headed for the kitchen. Constance had only to wait. Though, in truth, she was not much better at it than his Lordship was proving to be.

The milkman was about to tear his hat apart; he fussed with it so much. He turned it over and over in his hand, his eyes refusing to meet hers.

"Mr. Willace," Constance smiled and tried her best to comfort him, but his nervousness was evident. "Thank you for coming here today."

"The...your man said it was urgent, my Lady...."

"I'm not a Lady, just a woman. You can call me Miss Wellington." There, that should put him more at ease.

"Yes, Miss." He spun the hat faster now. So much for putting him at ease. "If 'tis the milk, I swear that it was fresh this morning...."

"No, the milk was quite fine...."

"The butter then? My wife churned it herself; she did. I..."

"Mr. Willace! Please." Constance took a breath. "All I want to know is if you spoke to a young Lady yestermorning as you made your delivery."

The silence that followed that question was answer enough. "You did." She made it a statement, not a question.

"Yes, Miss." He sounded so miserable, her heart went out to him, but she was closer to the truth, and her excitement was too hard to restrain. James, who had insisted on being there for the questioning, showed surprise at the admission, but said nothing. Constance began to think that the butler wanted to be there more from curiosity than to protect her from the man.

"When was this?"

"Just before dawn, my lad... Miss. 'Tis when I come here, you see."

"Cook would be the only one awake then," James added as an aside.

"Did this Lady give you anything?" Constance asked the milkman. "A letter or a parcel?"

Again, the man was reluctant to answer, but after a moment, he reached into the pocket of his trousers and pulled out something in a clenched fist. Slowly, his fingers uncurled and in his palm was a shining coin, a half-crown, more than a man in his position would typically save in a year.

He held it out to her, and she realized his hesitation. "I am not taking it from you. Truly, it is yours." His face lit up at that, and his hand flashed back to the pocket. "What I want to know is why she gave the coin to you."

"For arranging a carriage, Miss. She asked me if I knew of any for hire, and I told her that there's a man in town who has one, and he rents out the like. So, she gives me this and tells me to run to town and tell the man he's got a fare." He snapped his mouth shut, and his eyes grew wide. "Did I do something bad, Miss?"

Constance took hold of James' arm, ignoring the man's usual reluctance to touch. "James. Fetch Lord Allington. Quickly."

"Er...Earl?" The milkman took a step back and nearly knocked over a vase. "I'm no ways dressed to speak to a Lord!"

"You are, and you will," Constance stated as flatly as she could. "You will tell him exactly what you told me."

"Yes, Miss."

A door slammed. Running feet wearing heavy boots came closer.

The man coughed nervously. "Will he be angry, Miss?"

"On the contrary," Constance assured him, "you might just be the high point of his day."

CHAPTER 8

Burden of Companionship

L ord Allington could not stand another moment of idleness.
There was a trail to follow now, thanks to the cleverness of a
beautiful woman. When she had the milkman repeat his
encounter with Penelope, William was so relieved to have a direction to
follow, he'd hugged the girl without thinking. Not that he regretted it.
She fit well into his arms, but it wasn't proper. James pretended to look
in the other direction. The poor milkman just gaped about him.

William had given the man two crowns as a reward for his information, and the man nearly fell over from shock. He ran from the kitchens
to the stables. There, he saddled his own horse, much to the horror of
the stable hands. After a morning of forced inactivity, he must be away
and had no patience waiting on others.

Now, the horse danced under him, feeling the urgency. He spun the
mount around and called "HAH!" and let the horse spring under him,
riding hard and fast to town.

As the road disappeared under his horse's bounding strides, his
mind wandered between two women: his errant daughter, and the clever
Miss Wellington. He reminded himself she was a Lady's companion.
When this was over, he must have a conversation with her. Perhaps she
would be good for Penelope, to help tame the girl.

When he reached the house that the milkman had indicated, he threw himself from his horse and pounded on the door. An elderly woman answered and gasped as she saw who it was that cooled his heels on her step.

"Sire?"

"Good woman, I must speak with your husband. Is he about?"

"I...he's...I...."

Allington spun at the sound of hoofbeats behind him. *Excellent, the man is returning.* But it wasn't the coachman at all. A quite different figure approached, her eyes sparkling with fierce determination. "What are you doing here?"

"Helping." Constance slipped off of her saddle effortlessly as though she were made for riding. "Mrs. Hastings, is it?" She ignored him and went straight to the door. The old woman seemed to be trying to tell herself her eyes were actually seeing a Lord and Lady at her door. Constance ignored her silence. "Mrs Hastings, we have been told that your husband hires out...."

"He's not here. He's gone on a fare, you see. To Westlyham."

"Westlyham?" The word tore through William like a hot knife. He groaned. It all made a dark sort of sense. Constance gave him a quizzical look, but the old woman, Mrs. Hastings, wasn't finished.

"He should be back by now. It was a good fare, a Lady, like. I suspect though she paid him well enough, he's under a bar somewhere celebrating the tip." She blinked as though she'd said too much. "He said he'd be back last night; I'm sure he'll be along...."

Allington couldn't wait around any longer. He gave a coin to the old woman without looking to see which one it was. Given her gasp, it was probably a more considerable amount than he'd intended. Not that it mattered. Nothing mattered. He dashed to where his horse was gently grooming the other. He was only peripherally aware of someone beside him.

"You should return home." He spoke over his shoulder as he mounted. "I will send word."

"And I will be a witness." Constance was already in the saddle, her mare prancing beside his. "Wagging tongues will wag less if there is a woman present to escort the young Lady."

William laughed as he spurred the horse into a gallop. "Then they'll wag about you, alone with me, unescorted. You know what they will say about your reputation."

"I am a paid companion. I have no reputation to besmirch. Besides..." she spurred her horse and ran past him, "I am a better rider."

He would have liked to argue that but let it go. It was true, despite the amount of time he'd spent in the saddle, Constance was, in fact, the superior rider. Constance became a part of the horse, smoothly taking the gaits as though born to it. Even riding side-saddle as she was, there was a natural ability that was beautiful to watch.

Hours later, as the horses began to lather and tire. The riders were forced into a walk to let them rest. Westlyham was still many miles away, and the sun was at its height. William wasn't sure they would make it before dusk.

"What's in Westlyham?"

He pulled himself from his wool-gathering and turned to answer her. Even at a bouncing walk, she sat as elegantly as a bird. "Her maternal grandfather."

The word tasted terrible on his tongue, even just to say it. "He didn't...he refused to come to the funeral." The old anger resurfaced in him. "He disapproved of his daughter marrying a mere Baron. Even when my brother died, I wasn't good enough for his daughter." He tried to shake off the bitterness, but it weighed heavy on him. "Penelope was upset that her grandfather refused to speak to his daughter all those years and refused to be part of the funeral."

"If he was against the marriage," Constance said gently, "and you said that your marriage was unhappy...."

"Why did I marry someone I didn't like when I didn't have to?" William finished for her. "The old man did have a point. She could have married better, should have married better, but we were young, defiant, and she needed to get out from under his thumb. I needed a respectable bride. I suppose I tried to prove that I was every bit as good as my older brother."

He shook his head at the youth he'd been and bit his tongue against sharing even more. He'd already opened up too much to this stranger.

He startled when he felt a hand on his. Constance had moved her horse next to his, and, surprisingly, they weren't pushing each other to establish dominance as horses generally did. They seemed to walk companionably with each other.

Her hand was warm, and after a moment, he took it in his. They walked the horses like that for what seemed an eternity, hand in hand, as the horses caught their breath. If things were not so dire if they were not on such an urgent errand—

"WILLIAM!"

He jumped at the use of his first name and impropriety of the highest order, one that could have cost her life in a different age. When he saw where her finger was pointed, he forgot the breach of etiquette and spurred the horse savagely into a run.

CHAPTER 9

Under a Barouche

A single wagon wheel was poking up over the edge of a tree-lined drop. As William rode closer, more of the object came into view. It was the underside of a carriage. It lay nearly upside down at the side of the road, the top cover laying in a stream. A body sprawled close beside it; the splinter bars were shattered, and no horse was in sight.

They flew from their saddles. William reached the body first. It was an old man, his neck was turned around behind him, his expression one of shock and horror. Given how his neck was snapped, he hadn't suffered long, small mercy.

"William, help me!"

He ran to where Constance was kneeling in the mud, heedless of her skirts soaking up water from the river. She hovered over something... some*one*...

"Penelope!" He ran to the body of his daughter, his heart stopping as he fell to his knees beside her.

"She's alive, she's alive."

He almost didn't register what Constance was saying, but the relief was profound.

"Papa?" His little girl sobbed the word. It tore at his heart to hear it; she sounded so weak. "I'm sorry, Papa."

The arrogant, mocking "Father" she'd called him for too long was gone. She was his little girl again, and he wanted to hold her, keep her safe.

"I wanted to talk to Grandpapa..." she was crying now, "he wouldn't see me. I was coming back, truly I was, but the horse was spooked and... and...he's dead, isn't he?" William knew she was referring to the driver. Constance looked to him, her eyes filled with questions. He only nodded. Penelope sobbed harder.

"Shh, don't talk." Constance soothed the girl, stroking her hair. She'd pulled a cloth from somewhere and had wet it in the stream and daubed the girl's forehead.

"Why didn't you go for help?" William set his hand on his daughter's shoulder.

"I'm trapped." Penelope pointed down at her leg. It had been impossible to see because of her heavy skirts, but her ankle was trapped under the weight of the barouche. The fact that she was lying in mud was likely the only reason her ankle hadn't been crushed outright.

Thank God. Only pinned. If there was no break to the skin, she would likely not suffer infection. Nor die. To lose her...

He started up. "I must go and get help."

"The horses are blown," Constance shot back. "It's an hour each way on a fresh horse to the nearest help. We need to free her now."

"How?" he looked around for some indication of a way to help free his daughter. While he still had the strength of his youth, there was only one of him; the carriage was well trapped in the mud.

"I saw a hatchet under the driver's seat. Cut the spring free and use it as a lever."

He shook his head. "This is hanging on the edge of a ditch. If I lift that end, I may roll the entire barouche on top of her and crush her."

"It doesn't need to lift high, just an inch so she can pull her foot free." Constance grabbed his arm. "She's been out here all night. She's exhausted and been exposed. Please, trust me, I won't let it roll. Trust me."

He looked into her eyes for a long moment. Asking him to trust the life of his daughter to a woman he'd only just met was asking too much, but she was right. And time was of the essence. He nodded, and without thinking, he reached up and cupped her cheek in a familiar gesture.

She didn't seem to mind. She leaned into the caress and urged him to hurry.

CHAPTER 10

Bloom of Love

She looked at the barouche that loomed above them both as she heard the hatchet eat away at the spring. What had sounded a good idea was now frightening, to say the least. The girl was looking up at her; her sobs had subsided into small gasps for air.

Constance leaned over the girl, smoothing her wet hair back from her forehead. "It will be all right."

"Thank you."

Constance took the girl's hand in hers. "Of course." She smiled. "I look forward to getting to know you under better circumstances." As she said that, the sound of the spring cracking seemed to echo off the trees. It was time. She took a shaky breath, suddenly worried her plan was not as sound as she'd hoped it would be. "When I tell you to, you need to pull yourself out. Can you do that?"

The girl nodded, though she must have been weak as a kitten. "I shall try."

Constance nodded, in what she hoped was reassuring, and let go of the girl's hand to steady herself. "Hold on now." She heard the other end of the spring give way, and she dug her feet into the mud. She set her shoulder against the head iron, hoping that the piece supporting the roof would not buckle under her.

"Ready!" William called from the other side of the barouche.

"Ready." Constance braced herself against the metal and waited as the coach began to move. Penelope cried out as the wheel that trapped her moved across her leg, but, miracle of miracles, the wheel lifted just a little.

The weight on Constance's shoulder began to dig in through her dress.

It hurt. It hurt a great deal, and her feet began to slide in the thick mud. She couldn't hold it. She had been made to think she could, but the weight of it was making her slide, and soon she would fail. The ground under her would let her fall, and the barouche would roll over them both.

"FREE!" Penelope pulled her legs under her and rolled from the ditch and into the slow-moving stream.

"WILLIAM, STOP!" The barouche fell back with a thud. It slid down the bank, pressing Constance back until she fell over backwards into the stream next to the girl.

As one, they looked to the carriage looming over them. Constance held her breath, terrified that her suggestion would be the death of them. Oh, she'd been wrong to try it...

The barouche settled back into the mud with a creaking groan. It seemed to be in no mood to continue its descent. Constance and Penelope sat for a moment in silence, the water of the stream soaking them both. They erupted into laughter. It was a sound borne of nerves and relief and fear, but it was laughter, nonetheless.

Penelope wrapped her arms around her and held onto her tightly. Constance gathered the girl into her arms, not caring that they were both getting wet and filthy. She returned the hug freely and held her until William came splashing through the creek bed and wrapped them both in his embrace.

"Papa, I'm so sorry."

"Shhh," William whispered in his girl's ear. "Let's go home."

Ah, this was no place for her. Reluctantly, Constance pulled away from them, leaving father and daughter alone.

Only, William wouldn't hear of it.

"Come." He held a hand to her. Together, they helped Penelope to her feet. She limped, but her ankle wasn't broken. *Thank God.*

"You are as much a part of this as we are," he said softly, for Constance's ears only. To Penelope, he said, "May I finally introduce the Miss Constance Wellington. Without her assistance, you may well have perished in the countryside."

"Thank you," Penelope whispered, attempting some semblance of a curtsey. "It is a pleasure to meet you."

Epilogue

T wo Weeks Later

From there, everything seemed to happen rather quickly. Of course, this was entirely William's fault. Having found the love of his life, he had been loath to let her get away again. With this in mind, he set about having the banns read and making all arrangements post-haste.

At least his new bride had forgiven him for such a jumbled affair. As it was, even his children had been unable to attend the ceremony, both being laid up and recovering from their injuries. Penelope was up and about, using an attractive walking stick to advantage, having only sprained her ankle and not broken it during her escapades. Her brother had not been so lucky; the injury he'd suffered at playing cricket would entirely spoil his summer.

So it was that the wedding ceremony was performed quietly, with only the Vicar and his wife as a witness. They had decided to handle things peacefully. As William was so soon out of mourning and while Constance had no proper family of her own, such an affair was hardly worth notice. It was not as though he were well-titled or Constance of high consequence.

Sunningdale was where the actual celebration took place.

The wedding breakfast was considered the most essential part of the affair anyway, at least socially speaking. A handful of guests were all that was needed to make the experience a grand one, with much joy as the small family opened their arms to accept Constance as one of their own.

As William looked around the table, he could not help but feel deep contentment, alongside the eagerness to take his new bride home. Alas, they would have to wait until it was more comfortable for the young people to travel. Not to mention the problem of leaving Sunningdale entirely in the hands of the servants.

"I was asked to see to things here, William," Constance had reminded him gently when he brought the matter up. Not that he minded, for where she was is where he found joy.

He was not the only one enjoying the stay. Penelope was holding court at the foot of the table, surrounded by the friends she hadn't seen during her year of mourning. Constance had suggested she invite as many of her former friends to come calling to recount the story of her harrowing rescue. It had done much to alleviate the local gossip which had accompanied the mad search to find her. To be trapped for thirty hours under a conveyance was a subject of sympathy and horror. Penelope was still answering questions from doughty old women about surviving and being exposed to the elements for so long. To her father's dismay, she'd begun embellishing her story to entertain the curious and found quite a flair for storytelling.

He shook his head. Well, at least any of what would have been considered scandalous in the affair would be blown over by Fall. By the time Penelope would be presented by Lord Allington and his new wife. Thankfully.

Now, as he watched her, he could not help but feel a measure of pride in the young Lady. Penelope looked stunning. Her gown flowed out in every direction, reminding him of how quickly daughters grew up. She was a Lady. Soon enough, they would be planning her own wedding, especially given that Thompson Whelp had been following her about, seeing to a hundred small requests. The lad was Penelope's devoted admirer and trouble in the making.

Simon was little better, being coddled by any number of giggling young ladies who had somehow inveigled invitations to this special occasion. He shook his head.

As though perceiving his thoughts, Constance nudged him. He caught her grin and could not help but smile in return. None of these things was worth worrying about. This was his day. His and Constance's.

As he watched her now, making conversation with her neighbour, his heart soared. Things in their own household would be different now, of course, but different didn't mean bad. In fact, different could be quite good.

His face nearly split in two with the grin he tried and failed to suppress.

What was a wedding breakfast anyway when William only saw Constance? There was nothing else to look at, nothing worth his time or attention. Where he'd once married for convenience and prestige as a boy, he married now for love. Love had rooted in that fateful trip and blossomed in the time since.

As for the Ton, let the tongues wag. Maybe that was why he'd invited so many of them today, at a time when the more modest and quiet breakfast was more en vogue. Today, he would share his happiness with the world while letting them see the wonder that was his Constance.

Meanwhile, William saw nothing but his beloved's radiant smile and found he answered her with one of his own. Which was why he was so caught off guard by the arrival of a late guest. Or pair of guests.

"Constance?"

His new wife looked for a moment as if she might faint as she took in the slim figure at the doorway, resplendent lavender gown with a hat to match. "Arabella?"

He watched as his wife dashed to embrace her former ward. If his heart soared to think their visit would not last much longer now that they could soon go home to his own Estate, perhaps he could be forgiven. But while the astonished couple were only just returning home from their honeymoon, he could think of nothing more than how much he wished to begin his own.

To his joy, the look upon her face told him she felt precisely the same way.

The End

Eloping with The Lady

THE LADY SERIES BOOK FOUR

CHAPTER 1

Portrait of a Lady

The Sunningdale Ballroom had never looked so beautiful. After a year of mourning for the late Duke, it seemed to sparkle even brighter than before. When the ball had been announced, the news had brought joy not only to the ladies of the house, but to the whole of high Society. Indeed, it was the talk of the *Ton*. It had also sent the servants into a frenzy. Their mistress, the Countess, was a hard taskmaster, and they were eager to please or appease her, such as it was.

Distinguished gentlemen crowded the darkened windows and huffed importantly into their pipes. Their wives flitted about the ballroom like tufts of down battering in the breeze in search of eligible men for their anxious daughters.

Prunella took in the bright dresses and dour suits as they spun around her. She had waited for this moment for what had seemed like forever. She could see her sister, Arabella, peeking out from behind the tapestries. At sixteen, she was not yet allowed to attend balls. Prunella recognized the look of awe and longing she wore. She remembered it well.

Yet, here she was, dancing with a dashing young man at her very own coming-out ball, and the experience was not quite as magical as it had appeared from behind those tapestries.

For one thing, the gown was heavy, the corset was terribly tight, and her shoes pinched her feet. For another, her current dance partner, Lord Anthony Barlow, a minor noble her mother was enthralled with, seemed more intent on observing the room than he was in keeping up polite conversation with her.

He was a rather pleasant chap, in a perfection-carved-from-marble, would-faint-at-a-speck-of-dirt sort of way. He danced well, and while his ramrod-straight back and upturned nose should have indicated his good breeding, they left her somewhat unenchanted. She caught a glimpse of her mother standing in a circle of married women. Her mama was watching her every move.

Oh, please let this end soon.

God seemed to be in the mood to answer prayers that evening. The musicians mercifully ended the piece.

"You dance rather well," Anthony bowed to her and yet still managed to look down his nose at her. His smile was the perfect example of a grin, had it reached his eyes, it might have been pleasant. As it was, it was best described as predatory.

"As do you, Sir." Prunella dropped a curtsy. From the corner of her eye, she could see her mother mimicking the gesture, guiding her from across the room. "I think I shall need some refreshment." She smiled sweetly at Anthony. The effort was wasted. His eyes were not upon her but were searching the gathered crowd as though looking for his next dance partner.

"If you must," he replied absently as he nodded to one acquaintance or another.

She waited another moment for him to take the hint and fetch her some punch. Prunella came to realize that not only was he ignoring her needs, but he was snubbing her very publicly. More likely, he'd forgotten she was there. Such was the hazard of dancing with a boy you grew up with. Fuming, she turned and headed for the table, abandoning her escort in the centre of the room.

"Of course, her parents were livid," said Geneviève, one of the prettier girls in attendance. She was holding court near the punch bowl and had the group enthralled. "But she married for love." There were sighs of envy from every Lady in attendance, including Prunella.

"A love match?" asked a girl Prunella didn't know.

"What a scandal!" twittered another.

"It worked out well enough. He was a good match, though perhaps not so high ranking as her Mama would have hoped, but the income was sufficient," Genevieve conceded, as if she knew it took the sting from her story.

Prunella blinked and wondered if she could somehow insert herself into the conversation and find out just who they were talking about. Love matches were rare things in a London ballroom.

"Prunella." Her mother's voice cut through the gossip, and the young women turned and curtsied in unison to the Countess of Sunningdale as she came to stand behind Prunella. The girls took one look at her dour expression and scattered.

"What are you doing here alone? It is your coming-out ball; you should be dancing with every available gentleman. It is a monumental step in a young Lady's life. Do not waste the opportunity."

"I just needed something to drink, Mother." Prunella reached for the glasses. "I have been dancing all night, and I am quite parched."

"Lord Anthony is certainly a charming young man," her mother said softly, taking a glass for herself and using it to point at the object of her delight. For his part, Anthony was gathering his cadre of young men and seemed to be lording over them all. It reminded Prunella of the Reverend Perkins giving a sermon.

"Mother," Prunella chose her words carefully, "must I find a match this Season? That is, could I not delay until a love match may be secured?"

It was a daring question. She had always done exactly as her mother instructed. She'd prided herself on exceeding everyone's expectations, ensuring she was a fine example for her younger siblings. The mere suggestion of doing something of her own accord took a great deal of courage and no small defiance.

Her mother's eyes widened, and the glass she was raising to her lips froze in mid-air. The Countess turned slowly toward her daughter, and, for a moment, Prunella remembered all the reasons why she'd always done as she was told. Her heart quailed within her at the purpling of her mother's face, and she had a strong desire to flee. But there was no escaping this malaise.

"My dear, you will come to love the man you marry as I had," she said, an icy smile pasted upon her face for onlookers' benefit. The words, innocuous enough, made like icy fingers running down Prunella's back. They were not the comforting words of a loving mother; this was an order to be obeyed.

Do your duty. Marry well. Produce heirs.

The words had been drilled into her brain from infancy. She had never questioned her place in the world. But now that she knew there was an alternative to being married off to the highest bidder, she wasn't sure she could continue the charade.

She couldn't bear to stay for another minute, with Lord Anthony smiling benignly at her from across the room. Between her mama's machinations, the gossiping girls, and the rib-crushing apparel, Prunella had had enough of the festivities and of doing what she was told. This was her coming-out ball. While she could not precisely leave, there was no reason to subject herself to further discomfort, especially when she saw her mother making a beeline for the young Lord Barlow.

Her intent was clear enough; her mother would have Prunella dance twice in a row with Anthony Barlow. She might as well announce her betrothal to the man. It was too much to bear, especially as Anthony was nodding and smiling at whatever the Countess was telling him.

When she saw her mother grab hold of Anthony's arm and steer him towards her, Prunella turned on her heels and fled in the opposite direction.

A sudden blue wall immediately halted Prunella's progress. The wall turned out to be a man in uniform. Clearly no longer a boy, this particular gentleman was broad-shouldered and tall....and carefully avoiding the splash of tea she'd knocked from his cup. She gasped an apology and continued. Though not before locking eyes with the brightest, most intense green eyes she had ever seen.

She retreated to the shadows of the nearby curtains to give the man time to storm off in a snit, or die of old age, whatever came first. Though he seemed more intrigued than bothered by the ordeal. Perhaps she should have stayed and apologized more profusely, but she didn't know the man. And it wouldn't do well to be found in conversation with a stranger when her mother and Anthony caught up to her.

From her hiding spot, she could observe their progression through the room, puzzled looks on their faces as they searched for her. She giggled to herself and nearly leapt out of her bodice when she heard a throat being cleared in her vicinity.

Placing a hand to her heart, she turned to find green eyes and a blue uniform standing before her, hands clasped behind his tall, handsome back. The officer was smiling pleasantly at her. His eyes twinkled with either amusement or mischief. Prunella wasn't sure which. Beside him stood William, a neighbour she had danced with earlier. He was clearly uncomfortable from the way he tugged at his cravat.

"Miss Prunella Allington, may I have the honour of introducing Captain George Fitzsimmons?" William bowed stiffly, and his eyes kept flashing to Lord Barlow as though he were doing something clandestine. In all likelihood, he was. This was undoubtedly an uncommon introduction.

"Miss Allington." The officer took her gloved hand almost reverently, "I am enchanted to make your acquaintance."

Most uncommon indeed.

CHAPTER 2

An Officer, Not a Gentleman

Prunella wasn't entirely sure how the transition from a muttered introduction to a turn on the dance floor happened so quickly and smoothly. In a matter of moments, she found herself being led to the floor on the arm of the handsome Captain.

Her mother, brought up short by this sudden shift in attention, eyed the officer. Her gaze indicated she had yet to determine if the man was an interloper or possibly a step up from Lord Barlow.

Lord Barlow had no such doubts. The sour expression on his carefully schooled features revealed little patience for the man who stole away his prize. He'd lost his chance to secure a match quickly.

As for the Captain, Prunella was unable to determine his age. He was older than the ones who crowded around her before Anthony Barlow chased them away. He was tall, strong, and an able dancer. Beyond his green eyes and delightful French accent, the most striking thing about him was his smile. He never seemed to part with it. It was a genuine smile, like the Captain found joy everywhere he went. Surely, that was odd for a soldier who had seen the horrors of battle.

"May I congratulate you, Miss Allington," he said as he lifted Prunella's hand and brought her around in the dance. A dozen other girls copied the moves, their skirts rustling, slippers whispering across the floor.

"Congratulate me?" she replied. For a moment, Prunella couldn't imagine what he would have to congratulate her for. It belatedly occurred to her that it was her coming-out ball. Perhaps that was what he meant.

"You have truly captured one of the King's officers. That is not an accomplishment to take lightly."

"How do you mean, Sir?" She was genuinely puzzled. She turned and joined the other ladies stepping away from their partners and returning.

"That rather tactically timed approach when you upset my teacup. It was perfectly executed and quite effective." His smile wasn't mocking, not precisely. But he seemed to be sure that there was a joke being played, and he wanted her to know that he was aware of it.

She stared at him, her smile faltering. She was not altogether sure whether she liked where this was going. "I beg your pardon, Sir?"

"Oh, do not deny it. I was quite flattered."

Prunella was so shocked; she forgot to be angry. "Sir," she said as reprovingly as she could manage, though she winced when she sounded very much like her mother. "I can assure you that I accosted you entirely by accident. The incident should be attributed to mere clumsiness on my part."

As if to underscore her remarks, she threw his hand down, even though she was supposed to be holding it for this particular pass. "Come now, Miss Allington. You would have me believe that such a graceful dancer can be the victim of clumsiness? I cannot credit it," he smiled, reaching for her hand.

As her face grew hot, Prunella gave a short curtsy and said, "Thank you for the dance." When she turned to walk away, he caught her hand and pulled her back, twirling her to the beat. The other women on the dance floor twirled, skirts wrapping around the stolid legs of their male partners. She stumbled a bit as her feet adjusted to the change in direction, but outwardly, it only appeared that she had missed a dance step somewhere.

"I'm sure that on the eve of your introduction to Society, you would not wish to spoil the affair by causing a scene. It is so easy to cause a scandal these days."

She wanted to kick him, to wipe that smug smile off of his face. It did not help that he was entirely correct. By ignoring her put down, he'd saved her from making a terrible faux pas. She looked to her mother for help, but the Countess was eyeing Captain Fitzsimmons with the practised eye of a jeweller assessing a new stone.

"May I assume that the woman even now sizing up my coffin is your mother?" He twirled her rather vigorously, more so than the dance merited. She had no choice but to keep her attention on his face lest he send her flying. "Why do you keep looking at your Mama? Can you not think for yourself?"

"What?" Prunella felt the anger now. It radiated from her neck and began to creep into her cheeks.

"Are you of those girls who dare not take a breath without their Mama's permission. You are not one among their number, are you?"

"How...dare..." She could barely choke out the words; she was so furious.

"Which leads to an interesting thought. If you wished to save time, you could perhaps try dancing with your mother and leave me out of the matter altogether."

"Those are not the words of a true gentleman, *Sir*." She nearly spat those words at him. The musicians stopped playing at just the right moment for her to be easily heard by everyone on the dance floor, and then some.

"Touché, Madame." Captain Fitzsimmons clicked his heels together and bowed. His infernal grin followed her from the floor.

"Who was that?" Her mother intercepted her, her steely tone betraying the smile she held into place. She stalked from the dance floor with her daughter, leading her to a discrete pair of chairs where they might talk. "You left young Barlow without a partner. And for what? How do you know this man? Were you properly introduced? What is his breeding? His prospects?" Her mother chattered on—one question dovetailing after the next without a pause to answer any of them.

"Ladies and Gentlemen!" A resonant voice shouted over the crowd, stilling the flow of questions and saving her what was sure to become yet another argument. "Dinner is served."

Prunella turned to her mother, grateful to get a word in. "Mother, I did not accept a second dance from Lord Barlow. If that was his intent, he did not share it with me. Yes, I was introduced to Captain George Fitzsimmons by William, the second son of Duke Emery. As for the rest, it will have to wait until after dinner."

The Countess was about to ask more questions, but they were soon caught in the wave of guests filing into the formal dining room. She had no choice but to let the matter go.

"I have taken great pains to set Lord Barlow across from you at the table." Her mother hissed into her ear as they entered the dining room. "Do not disappoint."

Well, maybe it was not possible for her let the entire matter go.

Being seated across from Lord Barlow meant that Prunella was not in earshot of her mother sitting further down the table. Thank heavens for small favours. She settled into her chair and offered her most engaging smile to Lord Barlow. His spirits immediately improved upon receiving her undivided attention.

His face clouded over, however, when a strong hand grasped the chair next to hers. Out of the corner of her eye, she glimpsed the blue uniform.

"I believe I have been assigned this seat," said Captain Fitzsimmons, grinning as he settled in the chair next to Prunella.

CHAPTER 3

Dinner with a side of Mirth

P runella sat rigidly in her chair, back straight, chin up, and making sure her smile did not falter. Mayhap she hovered closer to the edge of the chair than manners dictated. So long as she didn't make it evident that she wanted nothing more than for this meal to end, she could make her escape later without causing a scene.

She introduced the gentlemen hastily and was rewarded for this social nicety by them speaking to each other while she composed herself.

It was challenging to relax with Captain Fitzsimmons so close beside her. She could feel his warmth at her elbow in a way that did not make sense. Lord Barlow certainly didn't distract her in this way, nor was she nearly as aware of him as she was of the Captain. Barlow was quite easy to forget entirely, even though he would not stop talking.

Lord Barlow was babbling away in a rather desperate attempt to impress her. Or perhaps he was trying to impress the good Captain, for his entire conversation seemed directed at him for some reason.

"Of course, as you doubtless know, my Grandfather was a rather famous military hero." Anthony paused for his audience to be suitably impressed. He waited in vain. In truth, Prunella could not imagine what the grandfather's deeds had to do with the stature of the man seated across from her.

Captain Fitzsimmons seemed to agree with her. "I was not aware." The Captain spoke politely, though his expression was one of suppressed humour. The man seemed ready to laugh at anything.

It was quite an unusual reaction to the world around them. Prunella glanced around the table at the other expressions, which seemed to speak more of boredom than amusement. Was every member of the Ton so jaded? Was she?

Lord Barlow kept talking, unaware of his intended audience's utter disinterest in him or the topic. The only person genuinely interested in what he had to say was the Lady seated beside him, who he mostly ignored as she was a married Lady.

"Oh, heavens, yes. He had a quite distinguished career." Lord Barlow launched into particulars, as though the war in question was of utmost importance and not one firmly decided more than thirty years prior.

"How beneficial for you to have an illustrious ancestor." The Captain said, interrupting the flow of information with a sly look at Prunella. "I fear I have only my own merits to recommend me."

Prunella shot the Captain a look, her eyes wide. How dare he insult a guest in such a way? Yet, if insult it was, the meat of it escaped his target. Lord Barlow looked pleased with himself, as though he'd been paid the highest compliment. Prunella's surprise transferred to him, shocked that he was so obtuse.

This was her mother's choice for her?

"Yes, we are quite proud of him indeed." Anthony was positively preening under the attention. He continued to brag about his family through the meal, embellishing upon every member of the previous generation; he had very little to say about himself.

When he began to shift his attention to a great-aunt, the creator of some rather witty rejoinder that had passed into the common parlance, Prunella stared into her soup and wondered if the interminable meal would never end. Prunella found it very difficult to pay attention to such a conversation. Her mind kept wandering. Beside her, the Captain daubed his lips with his napkin and muttered something about "watching a puppy learning to bark." It was all she could do to keep her spoon from wavering and spilling soup everywhere. She felt a laugh welling up inside her and covered it with a discrete cough.

Indeed, Lord Barlow seemed like a pup compared to Captain Fitzsimmons. It was even becoming harder to think of him by his title, the name Anthony seeming better suited to him. He was such a child in so many ways. Barely older than William, though younger than her brother Frederick. She was reasonably sure Frederick had more sense.

Were all eligible men like Anthony? She glanced around the table in dismay, noting, for the first time, the young men she was meant to choose from. How it was that her mother had allowed Captain Fitzsimmons to sit in such a place of honour was quite beyond her. From the look she was sending Prunella's way, it had not been intentional.

All these dreadful young men seemed inclined to model themselves after Lord Barlow. Prunella noted how they seemed to tie their cravats after the style he wore. They even adopted his mannerisms, that strange way he had of touching his hair as though to brush back a curl that was not there. What was that all about?

Nonsense. Prunella scolded herself for her frivolity. The young Barlow had pursued her since he had arrived. To suddenly side against him in favour of the rogue beside her seemed disloyal.

After all, he is my mother's choice.

She cleared her throat and forced herself to pay attention to what Anthony was saying. Meanwhile, the Captain kept whispering daring, and even witty, observations just under his breath. She didn't think he meant for her to overhear him. He seemed to be doing it for his amusement. The problem was that his commentary left her gasping, trying not to giggle in turns.

Goodness, if this keeps up, I shall be as silly as that sister of mine.

The other unfortunate thing was, that the Captain indeed was, more often than not, most correct in his observations. He was too amusing by far.

Her mother had raised her not to find things amusing.

When he complimented Anthony on his "dizzying genealogy," Prunella choked on her wine and went into paroxysms of coughing.

"Are you...quite well?" Lord Barlow interrupted his monotone retelling of something his ancestor had done and looked at her sharply as though piqued at being so rudely interrupted.

The gentleman on her left draped his napkin over his food as though she might ruin his dessert. From his appearance, she would have guessed that dessert was a favourite of his.

She glanced at him and smiled to show that she was done and indeed his raspberry ice was safe, when she caught sight of her mother wearing the most frightful expression. She seemed to be nudging her head in Prunella's direction. That she had an urgent matter for her daughter to carry out was obvious. What was less clear was the nature of the quest. Was it Anthony or the Captain she was supposed to address?

"Uh…" She glanced back at Anthony and then at the Captain, both of whom held concern in their expressions and then back at her mother. She couldn't interpret the grimace and the tight lips, but her mother's eyes flicked to Anthony and back again. It seemed to Prunella that her mother was trying to drag her daughter's eyes and lay them on young Barlow.

She nodded in understanding. "Oh!" She daubed her mouth then with her napkin, unconsciously mimicking the Captain. "I believe that I shall need a bit of air. I wonder," she leaned in and caught Anthony's eyes, "if you would be so good as to escort me through the gardens? I fear my coughing is disturbing the other guests…."

"Why yes!" Anthony tossed his napkin down over a half-eaten dessert. "I would be honoured." Though he looked startled at first, a huge smile split his face as he realized he had bested the Captain. The triumphant look he gave Captain Fitzsimmons was both juvenile and arrogant, and it made him look very much like a small dog receiving a treat.

She didn't appreciate this pompous display and would have sat down again if she could. As it was, she could only take the fool's arm when he came to collect her.

She stole a glance once more to her mother, who was deep in conversation with a Dowager on the merits of citrus fruit being imported from Spain.

"Your Mama will be pleased you followed her instructions." The

Captain said just loud enough for her to hear and turned back to his dessert. Prunella gasped and spun away from him, wishing she had a stinging retort for such impertinence. She took Anthony's elbow and left with the most eligible young man in the room.

Captain Fitzsimmons be damned.

CHAPTER 4

The Importance of Ribbons

"You and that Mr. Barlow were thickly in each other's company all night." Prunella's sister seemed unusually candid. The sisters were not often known to chatter so to one another. Arabella never had much use for Prunella, partly because Prunella had always been adamant about following her mother's rules, something Arabella did not necessarily excel at. But for some reason, the world of the Ton was fascinating to the girl.

Prunella ignored the comment and her sister's chatter.

"Do you like him?" Arabella pressed when she didn't respond. "I suspect you do; how can you not. He's the most eligible young man in our circle. Can you imagine being married to a man like him? I hear he is quite wealthy, or at least his family is. Did you know that his Great-Grandfather was rather well known?"

Prunella groaned inwardly. She knew more about Barlow's entire family than she could ever hope to forget. She turned and examined a bolt of cloth on a table next to her. She ran her gloved fingers through the weft and weave, not paying attention to the way it fell or the way it caught the light. It was merely an attempt to get her younger sister to stop niggling at her about the previous night.

"We simply strode around the gardens. Nothing was interesting about any of it," she said, hoping it would be the end of the matter.

"But did you not also dine in his company? I heard there was also a Captain at your side? What was his name?"

"I am sure I do not know what you mean." Her gloves were stripping the threads from the cloth. She was rubbing it so hard.

"I am certain you do. Were you not introduced to your table companion? I understand that he and Mr. Barlow had a lengthy discussion. However, no one can relate exactly the nature of the topic."

"Arabella." Prunella let the cloth drop back to the table. "The ball was last night. How could you have possibly had time to hear the gossip already?"

Arabella had the decency to look chastised, though her exuberance was far from squelched. "What I could not observe directly, I heard from the servants...."

"Arabella!" Prunella looked wildly to find their mother and breathed a sigh of relief when she saw that they had not been overheard. "Really!"

"And some I heard from Mother. She was pleased with the way the evening progressed, or so she said."

Prunella shook her head, inwardly she sighed. She needed to think, process all that happened, and not spend the day shopping and listening to her little sister. "But I also heard some of the ladies speaking in the other shops. They smile when they see you." Arabella's voice took on a pout, "they do not see me at all."

"That is just nonsense." Prunella tried to reprove her, but it was true enough. She had noticed the sly way the older women looked at her. Were she and Lord Barlow paired already in the minds of the ladies of the Ton? She wondered how she felt about that. It was one ball. It seemed too soon for such talk. It might be weeks before he asked for her hand. But if one listened to silly gossip the way Arabella did, in their minds, she had already married, passed through childrearing, and died together in their dotage.

It was a thought vile enough to make her stomach hurt.

Yet, as Arabella tried to extract more information from her, Prunella found her thoughts irrevocably returning to the Captain, as though she could take refuge in the memory of his smile.

Which was, of course, preposterous. The man was rude and quite likely a rake, given his easy smile. She snorted when she remembered how he had compared Lord Barlow to a horseflesh merchant boasting about lineage. To his credit, the Captain had been quite entertaining. Thankfully, Arabella had given up and moved to look at some ribbons.

Out of sorts and quite ready to go home where she might wrestle with her thoughts in peace, Prunella sought out their mother. After searching over the tops of more bolts of fabric, she found the Countess talking to a young clerk with great animation and high dudgeon.

"I ordered the ribbon last week! It is a critical time for my daughter, and I will not have her...."

Well, they certainly weren't going home anytime soon. Prunella knew this particular dance. Her mother would complain for another ten minutes, then demand to speak to whomever was in charge, start over, and then sit down and refuse to leave until the matter was made right. All this over ribbons? Prunella turned away and ran her hand over a delicate muslin as she turned this over in her mind.

Her mother was demanding, but why were ribbons so important? What was so critical about this time? She was launched, and successfully so. Was her mother now planning her courtship attire?

Had Anthony been that interested? He'd acted bored with her half the night. In all their years of forced togetherness, he'd never so much as intimated that he was considering making their association permanent.

She watched as the clerk bowed and scraped and tried to soothe her mother, but to little avail. She felt a kinship to the young man. Prunella had spent her life being biddable, polite, the perfect daughter and hadn't had any more luck measuring up than this poor chap.

Are you of those girls who dare not take a breath without their Mama's permission? The question still stung because it was true.

The Countess had her daughter's best interests at heart. But could Prunella spend her entire life based on her mother's decisions? It was a frightening question. What if her mother was wrong in the man she'd chosen for her daughter? Did mothers honestly know everything?

A love match. The thought kept creeping into her mind, forbidden yet alluring. It wasn't the proper way of doing things.

Proper. As if her mother were acting correctly now. Prunella tried not to hear the angry voice of her mother. The poor clerk had been replaced by an elderly gentleman who promised great strides in tracking down the ribbon in question and offered a replacement until it arrived. Arabella's head shot up at the mention of the other ribbon. It had obviously caught her eye. Still, their mother refused, saying that it didn't suit her daughter at all. As if Arabella didn't even exist.

Arabella also looked as though she wanted to bolt, though there was clearly no place to hide.

Prunella frowned at her sister. Must she be so dramatic?

She sighed. Once more, Prunella found her thoughts running for the sanctuary of the Captain's charm and wit. There was something to be said for rogues, especially clever ones who made her laugh. And he was right about that comment he'd made regarding Anthony's puppy state. It was rather plain to see the difference between them.

Perhaps Anthony only needed a little time? As he aged, he might mature and settle into himself. It was unfair to compare a boy to a man with years of experience behind him.

She grabbed her sister's arm and headed for the door. She needed to get out, to get some fresh air and hopefully, it would appear as though she was removing Arabella before the girl made a scene. Their mother was managing this entirely on her own.

Under her breath, she told Arabella to come along and be quiet for once in her life. The girl followed mutely, happy to escape the shop.

They didn't go far. When the girls had exited the shop, Prunella called to the footman waiting by the carriage and instructed him to go in and help the Countess carry their purchases. The man bowed and went in. Hopefully, his presence would cut short their mother's rant, and they could finally go home.

As they waited, Prunella wished she were brave enough to leave. But it seemed she was indeed afraid to breathe without her mother's permission.

CHAPTER 5

The Darkest Recess of Egypt

"I will stay behind with you. Let Arabella attend the lecture," said Prunella seeing her sister's crestfallen expression.

"She is too young and will likely get bored and disturb everyone with her incessant chatter," replied her mother. Harsh, but not altogether inaccurate.

The Countess lay back on the divan, her hand covering her eyes. "Besides, the lecture is not what is important. It is the opportunity to be seen and admired. Arabella will stay with me and tend to my headache." She uncovered her eyes for a moment and seemed to regret it instantly. "I shall be fine. Your brother, Frederick, can escort you."

She turned to look at Frederick, who leaned on the doorway, looking rather bored with the entire proceeding. "I am happy to do so, Mother, but if you and Arabella cannot attend...."

"Lord Barlow will be there!" Her mother snapped the words, her eyes flying open. She then moaned and fell back against the pillows, the very image of suffering. "Frederick, take her. Make sure she speaks to young Barlow." She waved off her eldest offspring with a finality that brooked no argument.

Arabella, absolutely seething at being left behind, threw herself into a chair near her mother. Like a petulant child, she made a face at them both as Frederick reached for Prunella's hand and tucked it in the crook of his arm.

~

The lecture on Egyptian artefacts was well-attended. Prunella thought her mother was correct in one thing: the lecture was an acceptable excuse to be seen. The topic was fascinating, and the lecture coincided with antiquities donated to the museum. Unfortunately, the elegance and pomp of the occasion were far more significant than a dry lecture merited.

Relating to pomp, she did indeed find Lord Anthony Barlow holding court with the young men. A bevy of girls, their skirts the colours of spring, drifted nearby like butterflies looking for a place to perch. He explained some bit of Egyptology, holding himself as an expert on the matter. In contrast, the others listened with great fascination.

Prunella snorted. By his own admission last night, Anthony had never travelled further than Paris.

Like seeing a great lighthouse on a foggy bank, Prunella nearly cheered when she saw her friend Constance in attendance with her companion and her father. "Frederick, I should very much like to sit with my friend and her family." He could take her words as a statement or question, as whatever suited him best. Apparently, either suited him just as well. He waved her off in the same manner as her mother had sent them to the lecture. His eye was already elsewhere, likely the refreshments and the wine offered there.

"Constance!"

Her friend turned and nearly launched herself with excitement upon seeing her. "Prunella! Do come to sit with us, say you will. Father arranged a box for us."

"I would love to," Prunella beamed at Constance. "And thank you for the invitation."

Prunella included Constance's companion in her thanks. The Lady smiled and introduced herself.

"The more, the merrier." Constance smiled and led the way up the steps to the box. "We have another guest with us today." She opened the door to show six chairs overlooking the stage. Half the seats were already occupied.

The men rose when the ladies entered. Constance's father greeted her amiably enough. But Prunella stood transfixed as she recognized the other man.

"Miss Prunella Allington, may I present Captain George Fitzsimmons." The Captain took Prunella's hand. She had begun to extend it before she realized who she was sharing the box with. The Captain grasped it before she could pull away. He brought the back of her hand to his lips.

"And, of course, you know his grace, the Duke of Wesley."

Constance's fiancé smiled and bowed. Prunella barely noticed him. Her polite curtsey was performed automatically, her mind still upon the way her hand still tingled where the Captain had touched her.

"Miss Allington and I are acquainted." Captain Fitzsimmons smiled at her. Prunella had forgotten how tall he was, though the intensity of those eyes had never left her thoughts.

"Oh, of course." Constance clapped, "from the other night at your coming out."

"Indeed." The Captain agreed with an easy smile.

Prunella realized they were waiting for her to say something. Oddly enough, she found herself bereft of her voice. She was shocked to see the Captain in attendance and with such great connections to recommend him. She no longer had to wonder how he had ended up at her ball. He was the Duke of Wesley's friend.

"Are you alright?" Constance set her hand on Prunella's arm. There was great concern in her voice.

Suddenly there was applause. A rather large man had walked out onto the stage. The group looked at one another, wondering where to sit. Constance sat upfront with her father. Miss Silver sat behind her and indicated that Prunella should join her. Once she was seated, however, Constance rose and asked Miss Silver to exchange seats with her. "I feel nauseous being so close to the railing," she claimed. Miss Sliver shot up and sat next to Lord Wellington.

But it wasn't Constance who sat next to Prunella; it was Captain

Fitzsimmons. When she frowned at the man, he nodded to the back row where Constance and the Duke were whispering to each other.

Of course.

Prunella smiled and turned her attention to the fellow on the stage.

"I have only just returned to England after adventuring to the darkest recesses of Egypt!" The speaker waved his arm expansively as if trying to encompass all of Egypt.

"There's a dark part?" Fitzsimmons whispered.

"It must have been at night," Prunella replied automatically. The Captain looked at her in surprise.

"Whatever did he do in the daytime then?"

"I would guess...." Prunella let the silence drag out as she carefully inspected the lecturer whose girth was indeed impressive, "eating."

The Captain nearly choked. Miss Silver glanced back at them, her expression unreadable. Prunella had no doubt she would hear about this later from her friend.

Prunella cleared her throat delicately and tried to listen to the lecture. Still, it wasn't easy to relax with the Captain next to her, who was trying, unsuccessfully, to keep his laughter in check.

When he made a quip about the mummified cat display, even Miss Silver had to fight to avoid laughing outright. She reached behind her with her fan without turning and smacked the Captain smartly across the knee.

When intermission mercifully allowed them a moment's respite for their humour, the Captain and Prunella rose immediately before Miss Silver could reprimand them for their inappropriate behaviour.

"I shall fetch us some refreshments." Captain Fitzsimmons offered as they descended the steps.

"We'll join you in a moment," replied Constance when the Duke made a similar offer. "I've forgotten my shawl in the box." The gentlemen bowed and left in search of cool drinks for the ladies.

Miss Silver and Lord Wellington were only joining them. Upon hearing that his daughter's shawl was left behind, he asked Miss Silver to fetch and went to the refreshment table to join the other men.

Constance captured Prunella's elbow and led her away so they wouldn't be overheard. "My dear, I have never seen you so...happy, so...animated."

"I'm generally happy...." Prunella objected.

"Not like this. I think it's wonderful." Prunella put a hand to her cheek and wondered if she genuinely was acting so differently.

"I must say I strenuously object!" The wheedling voice of Lord Anthony Barlow blundered through her thoughts like a dull axe.

She blinked a bit, having forgotten that he was in attendance. "I beg your pardon?"

"It is bad enough to spend such an excessive amount of time with that...that...soldier! But to carry on publicly. How does that make me look?"

Had she not been recently in the company of the Captain and if her friend had not just shed so much encouragement, perhaps Prunella would have been more circumspect. If her mother had been there, she would have submitted as she always had, but there was something in his tone that brought out her ire.

"Need I remind you, Sir, that you and I are not betrothed and that I am free to do as I please? We have known each other since infancy. If you had in any way intended to speak for me, you would have done so already on the strength of our previous acquaintance. Yet you have not. You have no claim on me whatsoever. Thus, it is none of your business whom I sit beside, whom I speak with or...or...." She searched for the rest of the sentence, her hands flying like distressed doves, "...or anything." She stormed off in the direction of the refreshments table, hoping to find her current escort. Constance, who had stepped away discreetly when Lord Barlow had started his tirade, could only shrug and follow her friend.

Captain Fitzsimmons was wending his way through the press of people and met her halfway. "Are you alright, Miss Allington?"

"Quite well." She took the proffered glass from him with a small curtsy and downed half the wine in a single gulp. "Yes, quite fine indeed. Shall we repair to our seats?" She tucked her hand through the crook of his elbow and allowed him to lead her back to the stairs.

"Certainly." Captain Fitzsimmons had indeed noted her change in mannerism, but she doubted he would find a reason for it. Anthony had hurried back to his group of admirers. The last Prunella had seen of him; his face held darkness like a storm cloud.

CHAPTER 6

A Gentlemen's Agreement

"Ah, young Frederick. So sorry your mother was unable to join us today!" Prunella turned to see her brother intercept Constance's father as they left the lecture hall. A man ran off to tell their coachmen to come and fetch the guests, and Prunella found herself laughing with her friend.

Captain Fitzsimmons and the Duke of Wesley were charming companions. The Captain had them all in stitches with his running commentaries and impressions. He was able to skewer the pomposity of the lecturer with alarming accuracy. Despite her spat with Anthony, the evening turned out more pleasant than she'd thought it would be.

Frederick gave her a conspiratorial wink. He never much cared for Anthony. Prunella was touched; her brother usually reserved these looks for Arabella. He kept up a conversation with Constance's father, who seemed very interested in Frederick's opinion regarding the lecturer.

"I say, Prune...Miss Allington," Anthony's voice cut through her humour. She found herself quailing at the sound. "A private word, if you please."

"Here, old man," The Duke of Wesley interjected, with a stern look at Anthony. "It is hardly seemly to wander off unescorted."

"Of course, Your Grace." Anthony sketched a bow and nearly missed it. The stench of wine was pungent on him, and Prunella suddenly realized her old playmate was well into his cups. To allow him to talk further with her escorts would invite a combative nature and resultant scandal.

"I believe we shall have more privacy over there," she pointed to the bench under the glow of gaslight. "It is, however, well-lit and within sight of everyone. I can see nothing so scandalous about a private conversation?" She aimed the question at Frederick.

"For Mother's sake," Frederick nodded, though none of the young men there seemed to care much for Anthony's interruption.

For mother's sake. He does this to make their mother happy. How many of us bend our lives for her happiness? And if that is so, why is it she is never satisfied?

These thoughts accompanied her to the bench, where she refused to sit. The coaches began to queue, each waiting while the one previously loaded its passengers, and the footmen secured the doors before advancing. She had no wish to delay her friends more than necessary; she knew they would insist upon waiting for her.

"I must admit, dearest Prunella, you have a cleverness I had not suspected. I applaud your resourcefulness."

Prunella searched the face of the young man for some clue as to what he meant. While it sounded like a compliment, something in the tone belied the thought. Was he accepting defeat?

"Whatever do you mean?"

"There's no need for coyness now that we are alone," Anthony said with a wink. "I understand why you did it, and I even accept some... small part in it." He held his finger and thumb apart to indicate how small he meant. "You were right, what you said back there. After all these years, I have not...formally...asked for your hand. I supposed... I naturally assumed that...well, your mother, for example, was so certain of us becoming...married...that it seemed like a *fait accompli*. After all, we are often thrown together at such...things...." He gestured to the lecture hall doors behind them, and she could see the flushed skin, the half-closed eyes. He had been into the wine. Well into it.

"You encouraged that old Captain's attention to make me jealous," he pressed on, "Well, you have succeeded, my dear. You have pressed me into a decision, and I have reached it. You want to be officially engaged, so therefore I am officially asking." He paused. "Here is where you say yes, that we might have the banns read."

He was proposing while drunk while omitting the actual proposal. After everything Prunella had endured, the man had waited until he was in his cups to ask for her hand. "Quit speaking nonsense," she snapped. "If you are in earnest, try again when you are quite yourself again."

"I am asking you to be my bride," he objected. "Is this not where your Mother's machinations have led? Can you tell me this is not what you have wanted all along?" He grabbed both of her arms and pulled her to him, his lips puckering and aiming for hers. She realized that he was about to kiss her publicly in front of both her friends and family. Neither of them could withstand that sort of scandal. Appalled and even somewhat frightened now, she pushed at his chest wildly, but he was stronger than she.

Prunella nearly lost her balance as Anthony was yanked away from her violently. Still holding a fistful of Anthony's jacket in one hand, Frederick ploughed a fist into Anthony's stomach. Prunella gasped and reached for something to steady her and found the stable arm of Captain Fitzsimmons.

Anthony landed in the ornamental bushes surrounding the lecture hall. Prunella looked for shocked members of the Ton, confident that this would be discussed the entire week, but most of the gathered had already left. The few who remained were dancing with impatience for their coaches and thankfully paid no attention to the gathered families on the corner.

Anthony came out of the bushes spitting leaves and covered in dirt with a twig sticking wildly out of his hair. "How dare you, Sir?" he snarled at Frederick. "How dare you lay hands upon my person? I demand satisfaction!"

"Get your satisfaction from me then." Captain Fitzsimmons wasn't finding this humorous at all. He clenched his fists now and would have charged the sputtering Anthony, had Frederick not held out a restraining arm.

"No, this is mine."

"I was but a moment behind you," the Captain protested. "It should have been me to teach this braggart some manners."

"SHE IS MY SISTER!" Frederick's face was beet red as he rounded on the Captain. "I know what I must do." He turned back to Anthony, who was nearly as red as her brother. "And it will bring me great pleasure."

Prunella searched their faces. Surely, they were not serious. She turned toward Constance's father for help but they too had left.

"Are you speaking of a *duel*?" Prunella's voice was barely a squeak as the import of what was happening struck her.

Her brother refused to answer her. George looked away. Anthony straightened his jacket and let her brother know that "arrangements" would be made with their seconds.

"Sir." Captain Fitzsimmons interjected when this aspect of things came up. "Forgive my impetuosity. I know that you and I have only recently met, but I would ask the honour of being your second in this matter."

Frederick looked at him for a long moment and nodded once, and turned toward Anthony, "Sirrah, this is my second. I will gladly meet you on the field of honour."

Anthony bristled at the name. "You shall have it, Sir." He stomped off into the night. His carriage was in the queue. The driver, seeing his charge wander off into the dark streets of London, pulled out of the row and followed his master. His bored expression indicated that he was used to this kind of behaviour from his master.

Prunella shook her head. Dimly she was aware of her brother's arm around her as she furiously blinked back tears. "Frederick, I cannot allow this. Please, do not do this. You are my brother!"

"Prunella, that is precisely why I must do it!" he replied.

"Do not worry, Miss Allington," the Captain said quietly, "It is all for show. Gentlemen meet, fire a shot into the air, and honour is satisfied. No one need get hurt."

"And if they are not 'gentlemen'?" She watched the back of Anthony's carriage vanish in the sparsely lit street. The Captain did not reply.

CHAPTER 7
A Matter of Honour

P runella waited in her room until the house was asleep. She knew that George, rather, Captain Fitzsimmons, was due at sunrise to collect Frederick for the outrageous duel. To her, it made no sense at all. No one had seen the indiscretion but her closest friends and family. No one saw Frederick punching Anthony. There was nothing to erase in the eyes of the Ton. There was no reason for this ridiculous duel other than some wounded pride. Surely, that was not worth anyone's life.

Sleep would not come. She slipped into a day dress and waited with nervous anticipation until the sky outside of her window began to lighten.

Carrying her shoes down the stairs as not to wake the household, and especially not her mother, she padded through dark hallways towards the door.

Gathering a cloak around her, she stopped to put on her shoes and slipped through the front door. On the way home, Frederick had proved adamantly opposed to listening to reason. Perhaps the Captain could convince him.

She quailed with the idea that her brother would be willing to die for her honour. It had never occurred to her before that he cared for her so deeply. The last thing she wanted was for her brother to lay down his life for her, especially over something so trivial.

She had to admit that she had not been the best sister a man could have, if only to herself. She didn't think she had been cruel to her siblings. At any rate, she fervently prayed that she had not. On the other hand, she had not been as demonstrative with her affection as she ought to have been. Yet the brother she had rarely thought of, except as a detriment to her freedom, was about to risk Barlow's musket ball for her sake.

Did the same hold true for Arabella? Well, maybe not. Sisters were different, weren't they?

She shook her head. She honestly did not know.

Guilt and fear warred with the brisk morning air as she gathered the cloak around her. The only hope, the only actual recourse she had, was in the hands of Captain Fitzsimmons. Of course, the very idea that the Captain insisted on defending her honour, risking his life for a relative stranger, seemed incredible.

As for Anthony – Lord Barlow – it was he who insisted on this act of barbarism to defend *his* honour, not hers. If there was one thing that settled the matter in her mind, it was that.

And yet, it had been her mother's wish that Prunella marry a man such as Lord Barlow. She pushed for it, though Frederick refused to divulge the night's events when they returned home the previous evening. Word had not yet reached the house of the duel, but no doubt her mother would be horrified when she learned of the matter.

Worse still, her mother did not care at all for Captain Fitzsimmons. She considered him flighty and unsuitable because he seemed to take very little seriously. Prunella almost wished she could tell her mother about the duel. The Captain was taking *that* seriously indeed. More so perhaps than Frederick.

He had tried to assure her that honour could be achieved without bloodshed. Still, she pointed out to him that both parties had to be honourable, and he was duelling with a man who had only family honour, none of his own. Frederick laughed at that characterization and tried to assure her that family honour would be enough. Brave, Anthony was not.

The dampness of the morning was seeping past the cloak and settling in her bones. She turned to retreat into the house. Perhaps if she waited by a window, she could spot the Captain.

She heard the creak of leather and the steady clomp of horse's hooves behind her. The Captain sat a magnificent horse, riding as if he were born to the saddle, he and the horse in utter harmony. He looked even more impressive in the pre-dawn light, his face a study in severity. He was leading another horse, one already saddled. That was for Frederick, and Prunella had a fleeting fear that her brother would return splayed over the saddle, his life's blood covering the horse's flank.

"Captain," she said as she stepped from the shadows of the porch and ran to where he dismounted.

"Miss Allington," the Captain seemed surprised to see her there. Was it so strange to be pleading for a brother's life?

"Captain, please. You must stop this."

Captain Fitzsimmons turned to the front door as if looking for her brother. "There is little I can do. In truth, had your brother not insisted on this course of action, I would have gladly taken the challenge on myself. I rather wish I could have, to be honest, but as your brother rightly pointed out, it was his duty."

"Anthon...Lord Barlow was in his cups. He cannot be held responsible for his actions."

The Captain shot her a look that she was sure had quelled many an argument on the battlefield. She could see the other side of the man, the severe soldier, a man hardened by conflict and war. She thought it would frighten her when she saw that side of him, the side she had always known was there. But it didn't. She found him tragic, in a way, as though his history had left an indelible mark, and she longed to be the one to erase that from his brow.

"Miss Allington, even when one is in his cups, one is still responsible for one's actions. Drunkenness is not an excuse to *assault* young ladies."

"But..." She bit her lip and thought of him and his uniform. "Is this what it is like for you?" she asked him, "being in the military, being at war? Never knowing if you will return? Is your life in danger so often that you offer it up so easily?"

The Captain's face broke into a big smile. "I do not offer to lay down my life on a whim, Miss Allington. Your honour is a grave matter indeed."

Prunella searched for a reply but could not find the words to address what had sounded like a flirtation.

"Prunella?" Frederick called from the front door. He closed the door quietly behind him, glad that his initial outburst had not awakened anyone. He said nothing more until he was close to where she stood with Captain and hissed. "What are you doing here? At this time of the morning? Unescorted and poorly shod!" He flashed a look to the Captain, who had the grace to look uncomfortable.

"I came to beg the Captain to put an end to this. Please! I cannot let you go through with this!"

"We have spoken about this all night, dear sister." Frederick sighed. "It was not I who insisted on a duel."

Prunella wrung her hands. Never had she felt so helpless. "Wait. That's it. Let me come with you. I can speak to him, make him retract the challenge. Barlow will admit that this was all his doing, that...."

"NO!" Though his voice was soft, her brother's tone was firm. "No. The files are no place for a Lady. Besides, do not concern yourself with such matters."

He mounted the horse, and after a moment's hesitation, the Captain climbed his.

"Are you serious, Frederick?" Prunella no longer cared about the volume of her voice. "Such matters? Frederick! THIS IS ALL ABOUT ME!"

Neither man answered her. In moments, the Captain and her brother were gone, and she stood in the gravel of the pathway, wrapped in a cloak and let the hot tears flow down her cheeks.

Her brother was riding off to die, and it was all her fault.

CHAPTER 8
Pistols at Dawn

Despite her resolve to wash her hands of the men, Prunella was unable to force the worry from her mind. The fear that her brother would not return was never far from her thoughts.

Of course, he would be the bigger man and shoot to miss, as the Captain had said. But what of Lord Barlow? Even if they both fired at the sky, duelling was highly illegal. If either of them, or their seconds, were indiscrete, it would go ill for the lot of them, including the Captain.

All this because of a failed kiss? All this because Lord Barlow was drunk. The man was a braggart and a fool, but he was harmless enough.

Captain Fitzsimmons. What was his name? George? George was an easy man with a ready smile. It seemed so strange to find such qualities in a military officer. Though had he been flirting with her at such a dreadful moment? Or had he merely hoped to lighten the mood?

With nothing left to do but to wait, Prunella found a place where she could sit and watch the lane.

When the servants came to light the fire, they were surprised to find her sitting in the front room. More than once, she had to assure them that she was fine, and that she did not require anything. So worried in fact that she became cross with the fourth maid who refused to take no for an answer. After that, she was undisturbed until Arabella awoke and found her sitting and staring out the window.

Whatever questions her sister had for her were easily ignored. Thankfully, Arabella gave up trying to talk to her and disappeared to the breakfast room. Prunella stayed where she was until she saw two riders approach at a fast clip. While they both rode hard, they were, thank heavens, both upright in the saddle. Prunella laughed in relief, but her humour died in her throat when she saw the looks on their faces. These were not the expressions of men who had won the day.

They jumped from their horses and tossed the reins to a footman who arrived running, his coat disarranged. They stormed into the house, and Prunella's fist flew to her mouth.

"Is that...blood?" She gasped and pointed to the bright red stain on Frederick's coat.

"It's not mine," Frederick said as he passed her and headed to the stairs. Captain Fitzsimmons stood at the base of the stairs looking after the retreating Frederick with pain and trouble in his eyes.

"Is he...dead?" Prunella asked. "Did Frederick kill Lord Barlow?"

"No, the young Lord is not dead." Captain Fitzsimmons shook his head. "Frederick allowed Barlow to take the first shot, and he fired into the air, leaving the matter settled. Your brother had intended to emulate the gesture, but as Frederick raised his weapon, he was startled by someone coming to tell us the duel had been found out. He tripped in his haste to escape, and as he fell, the pistol went off. The young Lord was wounded. I don't know how badly, but we must get your brother away."

"Away?" Arabella had just come into the hall, a piece of dry toast still clutched in her hand. "I heard voices...What's going on. Where is Frederick going?"

"Oh Arabella, now is not the time," Prunella snapped while at the same time George answered, "Your brother was involved in a duel."

"A duel!" Arabella exclaimed, her face going pale.

"Dueling is illegal, no matter what events led to it." The Captain told her, "whatever comes of Barlow, the fact that Frederick shot him may lead to an arrest. He needs to flee immediately."

"Frederick shot someone? What will we tell Mother?" Arabella turned to her sister.

"You will say nothing to Mother!" Prunella spat, and her little sister seemed to quail. "And you will *never* mention the Captain's involvement to anyone. Ever. If it were known that he was the second, his very livelihood would be at risk."

"Will you flee too then?" Arabella asked the Captain, eyes wide.

The Captain looked pointedly at Prunella. "No. There are some matters in London that require my attention and are worth the risk."

Prunella found herself blushing.

Arabella openly wept.

"Take heart." George took Prunella's hands in his. "I will see him safely to Paris. I will do that much for you. And for him."

Arabella nodded weakly. Prunella looked into the eyes of a man whom she was fast coming to respect and nodded. She felt her trust settle on his shoulders. She tried to smile but found herself unable. When Frederick went down the stairs with a single bag, no doubt hastily packed, she lost her resolve and fell into her brother's arms.

"I will see him safe." The Captain swore it as an oath as Frederick hugged each of his sisters to him. Without another word, the men took their leave.

CHAPTER 9

A Brother Lost

P runella smiled at the clerk and asked for six yards of fabric to be sent to the house. She added the ribbon her mother had wanted.

Her mother refused to shop, preferring to stay home. She prowled around the house, shouting at the servants, and even snarling at her daughters. Though she had no direct knowledge, there were rumours that Captain Fitzsimmons had gone with Frederick, making him the object of her ire *in absentia*.

She often fell into diatribes over the faults of military men. The Captain was wealthy, and a Lord in his own right. It did not appease her in the slightest. Her mind was set on Barlow and would not be swayed.

She had ordered and cajoled Prunella to make amends with Barlow, write to him, and beg him to accept their sincerest apologies. Out of desperation, Prunella told her mother about the assault in front of the lecture hall. This proved to be a mistake. Her mother fixated on the minor detail that Barlow *did* indeed propose to her.

"How could you? After all these years? All the sacrifices I made, the efforts I made to secure your future and finally, *finally*, he asks you to marry him, and you turn him down?" Her mother's face turned bright red, and she ended up shrieking before she was through.

Prunella stood aghast at her mother's tirade. "He tried to *kiss* me.

Publicly." Surely, the thought of a scandal would bring her mother around to her senses. Prunella had a fear of humiliation drilled into her from an early age.

"It is no scandal if you are engaged!" her mother fumed. "You should have said yes. This is about your brother. What did you do? What did you do to send your brother away?"

Prunella fled to her chamber and threw herself on the bed. She had never realized how petty her mother could be, how much she was a victim to the wiles of the Ton as Prunella was to her.

The thought made her ill. She carried on throughout her day, finding more and more excuses to shop or pay visits to friends. Constance was a lovely companion, and even Arabella joined her rather often, as if she too longed to escape her mother's sharp tongue.

Of Lord Barlow, there was no word. Rumour had it that he was "recuperating" at his home. Still, no one was entirely sure what ailment he was recovering from. At least Frederick had not killed him.

Prunella and Arabella maintained their regular schedules. Their absence, or a change of action, might precipitate rumour or, worse, launch an investigation into the constant talk that the young men were involved in a duel. Still, having no word from either her brother or the gallant Captain weighed heavily on her, and she retreated to her rooms as often as she could while at home.

She found herself alone in her rooms, thinking not of her brother but of the dashing Captain. The way his lips would rise before he said something that made her laugh, the way his eyes crinkled when he smiled.

She discovered she missed George dreadfully. And in her nightly prayers, his welfare was prominently mentioned.

It was a week before her mother could speak calmly, and then it was as though the entire incident had never happened. She was once more polite to the staff, at least as much as she ever was. They were once again attending soirees and balls, relying on Constance's father as their escort.

They had only just entered Lady Fendwith's ballroom when Prunella's mother caught her arm so tightly Prunella cried out.

"Look! Over there." She indicated the other side of the room with a tilt of her head. Lord Barlow was dancing with a young Lady and managing the complicated step rather adroitly. He may have bled on Frederick's coat, but he certainly had made up for the loss. He didn't even look as though he was inconvenienced. "That's Lord Barlow," her mother hissed uselessly. "There is still a chance. Go over there and ask for his forgiveness. Perhaps if you could get him to dance with you...."

Prunella could feel the blood rushing to her head. She could hear nothing but the way her heart pounded in her ears. After all this time, she had believed her mother had finally let go of the ridiculous dream of her and Barlow, and here she was back in the very same place.

"I will not!" She turned on her mother and pulled her arm free of her grasp. She found she cared little for who may hear her or what opinions would circulate through the Ton. "I would rather marry *anyone* else. I'd prefer to marry the next man I see than beg that oaf's forgiveness!" She spun around, intent on leaving the ball entirely. Let her mother marry Barlow if she liked him so much.

She was in such a state that she ran into the wall in uniform that was coming up behind her. She knew that wall.

"Captain Fitzsimmons?"

CHAPTER 10
A Groom Found

The Captain steadied her and released her. He wore the same mischievous smile he had on their first meeting. While she appreciated the irony, she was too breathless to remark upon it.

"I wonder, Miss Allington," the Captain said, his eyes twinkling with mirth. "Is that offer still open?"

"Offer?" Prunella tried to fathom what offer he referred to. For the life of her, she could not think what offer she had made to him.

"Marrying the next man you see?" the corners of his eyes began to crinkle again.

She grinned back at him, ignoring the withering looks her mother was giving the both of them. "And what if it is?" she challenged him.

"Well, Miss Allington." He took her hands in his. "I suspect that if such an offer were made, and if such an offer were accepted, then we might..." he looked over her head, and she could tell he was looking at her mother's scowl. The man was offering to marry her. If the Countess refused, and in such a public place, the resulting scandal, especially in the footsteps of the duel, would damage Arabella's future. She could not refuse, nor could she be prevailed to accept the sudden change in grooms.

"We might elope." He finished, pulling her out of the ballroom for a bit of privacy, though they were still in view of the Countess.

She did not resist. Indeed, she wanted to hold him and be held by him. "We might indeed," she whispered, as George bent down a placed a chase kiss upon her lips. It was exquisite. Though it lasted but a moment, Prunella knew instantly what all the fuss was about. Her entire being had come alive. Her eyes grew wide as she instinctively moved closer to George. Before she could kiss him again, her mother's voice cut through the blood pounding in Prunella's ears.

"Prunella!" she hissed and stomped her foot.

"Mother," Prunella said saucily, "there is no scandal if one is engaged."

Epilogue

"As Lord Barlow is unharmed," Prunella said, "and he has told no one of the duel, I think it would be safe enough for you to return home, brother." Prunella sat on a chair in an open café in Paris. Her brother sat across from her while her new husband was seated at her side.

Frederick smiled and nodded. "I shall, dear Prunella, but not just yet. I find Paris agrees with me. If I return now, I'll need to take on my father's title and duties. Those include finding a wife. I believe I'll enjoy my freedom for a while longer."

"Besides," Frederick leaned in and said in a conspiratorial fashion, "I am quite enjoying this side of you, sister." He raised his glass in a toast, and Prunella and George lifted their glasses as well.

Prunella placed a hand over her brother's, touched at the sentiment. She took a deep breath of the rain-washed air and took a careful sip. "Paris is lovely." She didn't say that the loveliest thing about Paris was how far away it was from their mother. She didn't need to; she was sure that was part of the allure for Frederick as well.

After spending some time in Frederick's company away from home, she was coming to find out many things about her siblings. First of which was how much she had alienated them by being their mother's perfect child. She intended to rectify that.

There would be considerable work to do if she wanted to build a relationship with Arabella. However, she had no doubt she could achieve it.

Wither George at her side, she felt as though she could do anything.

"Pardonne-moi un moment, ma chérie," said George as he excused himself and went into the restaurant. When they had arrived in Paris, George had reverted to his native French. Though he mainly spoke English to his bride, he was teaching her rudimentary French.

Frederick took the opportunity to query his sister. "Prunella. George is a good man, and I enjoy his company a good deal. But, are you happy?"

She grinned as large as her husband's best smile. "Oh yes. Very happy."

He chuckled at her enthusiasm. "If he is the reason for this happier, more relaxed version of my sister, then I cannot recommend him enough!"

"You didn't like the old one?" she teased, thinking how little she liked her old self in retrospect.

"On occasion," Frederick admitted with a small smile. Prunella's grin faded.

"I know I have not been the best of sisters," she admitted, "but I hope to make amends, somehow, to Arabella. And poor Henry whom I barely see or speak to."

"Arabella will forgive you easily," Frederick assured her, "as I have. And Henry craves attention. He will welcome any overture. I admit I might make more of an effort with him when I return."

Prunella reached across the table and grabbed her brother's hand. "I feel as though I have just awakened into a bigger world than I ever dreamed possible."

"Moi aussi," George said from behind her. He held a bouquet of roses out to her. "I saw a street vendor and knew they were for you."

Her face lit up at the romantic gesture. She buried her face into the sweet smell and soft petals.

Yes, indeed Paris was lovely. But then, any place she went with George Fitzsimmons would be paradise.

The End

Dancing with The Lady

THE LADY SERIES BOOK FIVE

CHAPTER 1

From One Friend to Another

The Dowager Countess of Sunningdale, Victoria Allington, watched the dancers with a careful, critical eye. The rustle of silk, the tempo of the tireless musicians, were mere artifice in the oldest of dances between men and women. Young women smiling encouragement to the young men who pursued them, the casual, innocent brush of limbs. Of course, the was always one or two couples who were brazen enough to *waltz*, a heathen ritual that disgraced both families of the impertinent couple.

Thank goodness her daughters were safely married. Though her duty was discharged, and the girls were satisfied with their choices, Victoria couldn't help feeling they might have done better for themselves had they listened to her sage advice.

She turned her eye to where they stood with their husbands. The four of them were laughing at some jest, likely told by Major Fitzsimmons, who never seemed to take anything seriously. What did such behaviour say about His Majesty's army that such a man was not only an officer but a recently promoted Major?

What was worse was that her son Henry had been unduly influenced by the man. He was even now in Paris finishing his studies with the full intent of entering into a military career when he was of age. Like all her children, he too could do better with his life, but he refused to listen to his poor mother, just like his siblings. She didn't even want to think of the bride Frederick had chosen. Though the girl was from a suitable background, she did not do the title justice.

She settled deeper into her chair, decidedly out of sorts and reminded herself that the Major wasn't a bad sort as far as a career soldier went. Certainly, Prunella seemed enamoured with him. She couldn't fault Arabella's choice; Viscount Pommeray was not only a respectable fellow, but he was also an excellent dancer.

She nearly jumped out of her skin when Lady Adeline Porter suddenly took the chair next to hers, a glass of punch cradled carefully in her hand. "They look happy."

Victoria returned her gaze to her daughters. "There is more to life than happiness." She sniffed. "I have dedicated my life to them, you know. I sacrificed and did everything in my power to ensure they had good lives."

Lady Porter nodded, a pleased smile on her face. "As do we all for our children. Congratulations, you seem to have done well enough."

"If I might be frank with you," Victoria leaned toward her friend, making sure there were no other ears within reach of gossip, "they have little respect for all I have done. They may be happy now, but they will eventually come to see the value of the matches I had made for them. The matches they *refused*. On that day, they will realise I only had their futures in mind."

Lady Porter's smile wavered until only one side of her lips curled up. "Tell me something, dear," she took another sip of her punch, her expression smoothing to something more neutral, "what exactly was it that happened to you?"

Lady Allington broke her gaze from her children and set it upon her friend, as if seeing her for the first time. "I have no idea what you mean."

"I have known you since we were both girls." Lady Porter finished her punch with a sudden swallow and placed the empty glass on the tray of a passing waiter. "I remember well when we were their age." She pointed toward the dancers. "You laughed nearly as much as those girls do now. You also got into a great deal of mischief, much to your father's consternation." She giggled and nudged the Dowager Countess with her shoulder. "In truth, you were a lot of fun to be around."

Lady Allington drew herself up stiffly. "I still am...."

"No. You are not. If you were, you would be over there with your children, basking in the glow of their admiration. Not standing here with another old woman who has too much time on her hands and not enough to occupy her decently."

"They just don't appreciate...." Lady Allington began.

Her old friend made a noise that might be considered rude. The guests nearest them turned to look. "That is a great load of wash water." Lady Porter's gaze was shrewd. "Tell me, are you settled now within the Dower House?"

"Finally." Lady Allington shivered at the memory. Was it so difficult to have the things put where they belonged? She had fussed and screamed at the help for what seemed hours before the place was put to rights. "It was...difficult to let go of the house I have lived in since my marriage, but I suppose that is the fate of the underappreciated mother."

"No." Lady Porter set one delicate hand on Allington's forearm. "That is the inevitable fate of a cranky old woman." She raised her voice slightly to be heard. "A fussy old woman who will likely *not* be invited to spend any time with her grandchildren."

A coldness crept over Lady Allington. This was something that had not occurred to her. "They would not dare." Even as she said it, a part of her mind recoiled at the thought. "Would they?"

"Dearest Victoria," Lady Porter sighed. Only a very intimate friend would dare call her by her given name. She suddenly felt as though she were being called on the carpet by the headmistress of the finishing school they had attended together so long ago. She felt her hackles rise. Wounded pride? Perhaps. Better that than being found in the wrong.

"I could also point out that *your* children, and their husbands, are on the opposite side of the room while you are sitting here with me," Lady Allington pointed out. A touch of anger creeping into her voice despite her best efforts to remain cordial.

"Only because I thought an old friend might need me. They will be delighted to welcome me back when our conversation is completed." Lady Porter rose carefully and shook out her skirts. "Can you say the same?" She lingered only long enough to give her old friend a strange look. To the Dowager Countess, it looked remarkably like pity. "I sorely miss the girl I once knew. I have waited so many years to see her again." Lady Porter shook her head sadly, as one might at a funeral. With a swish of her skirts, she wove her way through the crowded ballroom to join her family.

So it was that Lady Allington found herself alone in the ballroom. Even the press of the crowd seemed to have formed a pocket around her. It was a sad and miserable place to be.

To her consternation, she found she was less interested in the comings and goings of the dance and more concerned with her lack of Society. She had spent so many years finding the best matches and creating the best futures for her children. Matchmaking was a competitive business. She'd had no time to nurture her own acquaintances. It was just another area that she had sacrificed for her children.

Did she regret it? She straightened her back and held her head high, reminding herself that regret was a ridiculous conceit. She was a Countess. Her children, despite their impetuosity, had not made such poor showings that the Ton had an excuse to waggle a tongue. Nor had they disgraced the family name beyond repair, even if Frederick had created something of a scandal not all that long ago. These things were due to her skills in raising them as much as anything. Certainly, they knew that her advice, freely given, was intended for their betterment.

She strode across the floor with dignity and grace as befitted her station and headed directly for her daughters. Prunella saw her first. The laughter on her daughter's face fled as though it had never been. Prunella reached over to tap Arabella's arm. Here too, the laughter died as the two girls rose to meet their mother in much the same way a condemned man might rise to face a firing squad.

The gentlemen behind them, their husbands, rose too, as befitted gentlemen, but their posture was not one of gentility. Rather, theirs was a movement which spoke of protection, for they seemed ready to jump between her and her daughters, if necessary, to keep their ladies from harm.

Arabella dropped a perfunctory curtsey, and Prunella followed suit after a short hesitation. Had their mannerisms always seemed so begrudging, or was it their newly married status that embittered them so? Or, heaven forbid it, was there something to her friend's warnings?

"Are you enjoying the ball?" she asked, her tone stiff and polite.

"I'm sorry, Mother," Prunella said contritely. "I know it behoves a young Lady to mingle." She tugged the Major's sleeve and nodded toward where the dancers spun about the dance floor like so many butterflies trying to take flight. "Would you do the honour of escorting me to the dance floor? I believe they will be ending this set soon."

Arabella did not even bother with the pretence of asking. She simply turned and grabbed her husband's hand, nearly pulling him across several chairs to where the dancers were lining up for the next dance.

Lady Allington stood abandoned where they had left her. She faced a heavily curtained window, alone but for a handful of empty chairs. No one had witnessed her family fleeing at the sight of her. The music continued; men and women revelled in the dance and in each other. She was an island in a sea of gaiety with no sense of where she belonged. It was a strange and almost dizzying feeling.

Though the room was warm and filled with people, Lady Allington felt a sudden chill that caused her to wrap her arms around herself. She stood facing away from the dancers, pretending an interest in what lay on the other side of the glass. Not that she could see anything. Outside it was too dark and the ballroom too bright. She could not see a thing save her own reflection. Well, it was better than turning around and facing the pitying looks on the faces of those around her. Worse, she could not bear to look at Lady Porter again.

She had never been so humiliated in her life.

CHAPTER 2

The Girl You Once Were

I t was too early to visit; Lady Allington knew that. The ball had gone on long after she had made her excuses and left. This did not mean that others left when she did. Lady Porter was likely there until the wee hours, leaving as the sun rose and would be abed for the rest of the day.

But that was the problem, was it not? If Lady Allington could have slept at all, her old friend wouldn't have had a visitor at the horrible hour when the cocks had yet to clear their throats and breakfasts were yet to be made. Still, the servants were awake bustling from one chore to another at the hour she arrived, so it was not as though she were waking the entire household.

Yet, it had seemed as though God Himself had conspired to keep her from her oldest friend this morning. The coach wasn't ready when she wanted. The coachman couldn't be found. When he was finally located, she was only told he had returned, but no one would tell her *where* he had been. No doubt he had been enjoying a dalliance with a bit of muslin. She would see about that and let the girl go. Or rather, she corrected herself, ask her daughter to let the girl go. Even the servants were out of her hands now.

The ride to the Porter Estate was the coachman's revenge. Victoria would go to her grave, insisting that the man found every hole and rut the wheels could slide or slip into. By the time she got where she was going, she was sorely convinced that she was carrying more than one bruise. She had effectively been tossed around in the back of the carriage like unsecured luggage.

Either the driver, or the horse, might have been suffering from too much indulgence the night before. She hoped it was the driver because she was fond of horses and would hate to think poorly of the beast.

A footman wearing the livery of the Porter House rushed out to open her door and assist her down the carriage. When her feet were firmly on the ground, she stopped to catch her breath and thanked the Lord that she had survived the ordeal.

"See to it that my driver has some breakfast," she instructed the footman, "or have him shot. Use your best judgement." She straightened and strode deliberately to the door as the footman stood where she left him, his head swivelling between her and the bemused driver still perched upon the driving board.

At the door, the butler informed her that her Ladyship would be down shortly, indicating that Lady Porter had been asleep upon her arrival. In the meantime, she was invited to sit in the front room.

Apparently, her old friend was a heavy sleeper, for she was left to her devices for quite some time. It occurred to Lady Allington more than once to leave. But now that she was here and had already disturbed her hostess, it seemed more than a touch rude to depart without seeing her. Besides, as much as she hated to admit it, she was there in the role of the supplicant.

When Adeline Porter descended the main staircase, she was dressed, coiffed, and elegant as ever. It was only occasional yawns and the slight glaze in her eyes that betrayed her sleepy state.

The woman seemed to resurrect before her eyes, a bracing cup of tea and a few scones later. Apparently, the ball had been quite a success as the guests had stayed somewhat longer than was normally fashionable.

"Prunella conveyed your apologies," Lady Porter assured her around a flaky concoction made of flour and almonds. "I was sorry to hear that you had been taken by such a sudden headache. I trust you have recovered?"

Lady Allington watched her friend's face carefully. There was no doubt in her eyes that the headache had been merely a convenient excuse to flee the festivities. Considering the topic of the previous night, Adeline Porter had likely already formed the opinion that Victoria Allington had fled. Escaping not the party nor even the Ton, but her very own children.

Lady Allington saw no point in beating about the bush. "My children will be spending the Winter holidays at Sunningdale Manor. I've been invited to stay for the duration." She bit her lower lip and stared into the cold fireplace, not quite sure how to proceed.

Lady Porter's eyes were sympathetic. "My dear, do have a scone. Or one of those miniature pastries. They're quite good."

"No, thank you. I have...I have considered the advice you gave me last night."

"Oh, good heavens." Lady Porter placed her hand on her breast, "have I given advice? I must profusely apologise."

"No." Lady Allington shook her head. "You were...well, you seem to be...correct. I fear this will be a very bleak Christmas season, at least for me. I wonder if my children wouldn't have a merrier time without my... presence."

"Do not be ridiculous." Lady Porter snorted and contemplated another of the small tarts on the plate between them. "Your daughters care for you, and you know it. Christmas is a time for family and togeth-erness." She seemed to decide against the treat and resumed her tea. "Why would you think such a horrid thing?"

"There is some truth to your...warning." She was about to say "advice" again and only just caught herself in time. "I have seen it myself. Their happiness is fleeting when I approach. Their demeanour changes as though I were old Mrs. Winthrop."

"Oh, please do not even say that name." Adeline Porter shivered, her extra chin waggling with the memory. "And that...woman...was *evil*. You, my dear, are not."

"Maybe she only worried about what was best for her charges." Lady Allington turned toward her friend, reaching for her hand. "Could she have been just determined and just as...as *wrong* as I have been?"

"Good heavens, dear." Porter covered her friend's hand in hers. "You're not nearly so bad as all that."

"I am sure Mrs. Winthrop believed the same thing. Yet we both tremble at the memory of our Headmistress, all these years later. I do not want my children to refuse to say my name to avoid remembering me. I have no wish to lose whatever time I have been given with my future grandchildren because I have been...." She retrieved her hand and placed a gloved finger beneath her nose. Tears were threatening, and she could not bear to shed them.

"Then change, my dear." Lady Porter rose from her chair and came to sit beside her friend. The divan sagged a bit under the added weight. Victoria found herself naturally leaning into her, largely because Lady Porter was causing the furniture to buckle slightly. "I remember a young woman who laughed easily, who never walked anywhere she could run. I remember..."

"That was so long ago!"

"It was." Lady Porter sighed, her expression wistful. "Yet I am convinced that girl is still in there somewhere under rules and confines. If only your children knew *her*."

"But how? How does one resurrect the way one was before husbands and children, obligations, and heartbreak? It sounds easy enough, but I have been the way I am for far too long to revert to a girl I can scarcely remember."

"Nonsense. It really is quite a simple matter." Lady Porter ground her teeth together and pushed herself off the couch. "Here..." She picked up the little serving bell and headed to the small writing table. When the maid came, she called for foolscap and ink. "I shall write it down for you. It is simplicity itself."

She thought for a moment, wrote something, thought a moment again and added it to the list. "Here. Here are new rules for you to follow." She blotted the parchment and scattered sand upon it to dry it more quickly. "Though they may appear simple, you may struggle when first attempting them."

A twinkle in the large woman's eyes made Victoria wary. Adeline had been her friend, her only friend for many years. If she thought

Victoria should try, then try she would. Victoria missed the carefree girl she was once was.

She read the list.

- *Speak with kindness*
- *Try something new*
- *Enjoy the moment*
- *Look on the bright side*
- *Laugh more.*

"Do not attempt them all at once, dear. This is the sort of thing one wants to ease into."

Victoria Allington lifted her eyes from the page and searched her friend's eyes. She realised she was looking for reassurance that she could do any of these. After all, she was quite settled into her ways.

Lady Porter seemed to understand. Her face softened, and for a moment, she almost seemed like the friend she had been of old, the girl who had never once steered her wrong, whose counsel had gotten her out of more than one scrape. "You tell me often about the sacrifices you made for your children," she reminded her. "Make this one for yourself."

The Dowager Countess left with a sense of optimism she hadn't felt in years.

CHAPTER 3

The Boy He Used to Be

The driver had somewhat recovered by the time she returned to her carriage. The ride back to the townhouse was less of a quest for holes and ruts than the ride in. That suited the Dowager Countess, as she stared at the scrap of foolscap with her new list of rules.

The whole idea seemed foolish. Victoria wasn't a bad person, not like Mrs. Winthrop had been. Of course, being the headmistress of a school of unruly children would certainly turn anyone bitter. Certainly, the old lady hadn't been a saint, nor was she someone the children were particularly fond of. She *had* kept order and provided a solid education in etiquette and comportment. Most of her charges had made respectable matches and become respectable members of the Ton.

Now, as she journeyed home, Victoria tried to convey belated gratitude to a woman gone these thirty years or more. It occurred to her that she never knew when the old headmistress had passed away, nor had she cared. Looking back, she had shone no more appreciation for the woman's hard work than her own children had. Such was not a fitting legacy for anyone.

No mother, or grandmother, deserved to be so thoroughly forgotten.

The words on the paper swam under her gaze as though they

mocked her. As though she was incapable of kindness. She always spoke with kind intent. Perhaps it wasn't kindness, though. Wasn't it better to assist someone in correcting their mistakes than to be patronising, allowing others to gossip behind their back?

She folded the page and held it close to her breast, trying to remember who she had been in her youth. Adeline Porter was so enamoured with how she used to be. She was so certain that would be the key to bridging the divide with her children. It was only sensible to remember who that girl was herself.

The memories that surfaced seemed to be of a child with neither discipline nor self-control. The thought of running through hallways, hair loose around her shoulders...certainly she was not expected to take matters *that* far. She was a Countess, not some foolish child.

Adeline certainly was no longer capable of running. She could hardly expect Victoria to either. What else was there then? There were tricks played on the teachers, she supposed. Even Mrs. Winthrop herself had not been spared their mischief, though now their tricks seemed petty and ridiculous.

So, what was it then that was lost? Silliness? Foolishness? A lack of respect for her elders? Now, she was the elder. There seemed to be progressively fewer and fewer elders among her acquaintance.

She studied the list once more. It seemed deceptively simple, even childish. Once more, it was, decidedly, a list of things you might expect a girl who were not yet out in Society to do. While Victoria had admitted that she missed the girl she had once been, and even acknowledged there was a lightness to youth, she was beyond such carefree feelings.

How in the world was one expected to—

Her thoughts were rudely interrupted as the carriage began to buck wildly from side to side. The horse was screaming. She grabbed at the window, at the door, anything that would steady her. She could see hooves flashing as men shouted from somewhere nearby. The list flew from her grasp as she was violently thrown from one end of the carriage to the other.

Victoria saw another conveyance through the window of her carriage. Rising on her rear legs, the mare was trumpeting a challenge to the horse up ahead.

There were two men in the driver's seat of the other carriage, one dressed in the livery of a house, and an old man holding the reins. The first leapt off the board to calm the horses while the other struggled to hold the phaeton steady.

Victoria grasped the frame of her carriage and stared in wild wonder at the old man dressed like a gentleman. She would have known him anywhere, though how he came to be here defied all logic.

Apparently, her attempts at resurrecting her childhood had unexpected results. She had apparently summoned one Harold Livingstone.

Age had been kind to him. Though his thick, wavy black hair was now more silver than black, and his beard was full and iron. His eyes were still as bright as she remembered. If anything, he looked better than he had. Time had not diminished him one whit.

She tried to straighten her hair, but her horse would not be calmed, and the carriage rocked violently back and forth. Harold sent his man to assist with calming her horse, now that Harold's animal stood alert but quiet.

"My pardon."

Harold did not sound one whit apologetic. If anything, the ruddiness of his cheeks and the ready laugh showed him to be quite unrepentant. It was, in a way, refreshing to know that some things do not change. It was also extremely annoying.

"Madam," Harold tried to peer into the coach. "I beg your indulgence; I fear I let the horse have her head and could not control her enthusiasm for running." He leaned over further and shielded his eyes to better see into the interior of the coach. "Good God. Could it be? Victor...the Countess of Sunningdale?" He leaned back on the driving board, and the familiar booming laugh she had not heard in decades filled the space between them.

She clamped down her teeth and thought of a response that incorporated a questionable parentage while trying to demean oneself when one has a perfectly good driver *right there*! She reached down and snatched the paper from the floor of the carriage before it got misplaced.

Speak with kindness.

She swallowed the imprecations she had planned for burning his ears and took a deep breath. Kindness, was it?

"I am the Dowager Countess, now. I see that your ability to drive a carriage has transcended time itself."

Harold stared at her for a moment, a grin beginning to split the thick beard. He threw his head back, and the booming laughter did as much to calm her horse as his driver did.

She crumpled the note in her fist.

She may murder Adeline yet.

CHAPTER 4

Try Something New

"I decided to try out the horse." Lord Livingstone alit from the driver's seat and swaggered to where Victoria sat in the shadows of her carriage. "It's new, you see." He flashed her that same mischievous grin she remembered so well. "So is the carriage."

"I was under the impression you were still in India." *If you had been, you would not have driven me off the road.*

"I only recently returned." Livingstone leaned on the door. Impertinent as ever. She was essentially trapped now in her own conveyance. Of course, there was a door on the other side, but that was quite beside the point.

"So, then everything is new to you," she pointed out. "Does this mean you have the intention of burning down your house to determine its flammability?"

Harold grinned, his beard fairly bristling with humour. "I have given you a turn, my Lady." He sketched a perfunctory bow. "Please allow me to make things up to you. I shall be giving a lecture regarding the Indian Continent later this week. I would be honoured if you would attend as my honoured guest."

"Lord Livingstone..."

"Harold. Please. Like you used to call me."

"Lord Livingstone," she repeated his name as fiercely as she could manage while still giving the appearance of good manners. "You gave my horse a frightful turn. *I*, however, am fine."

"Then bring the horse!" Livingstone slapped the side of her carriage. "I shall arrange a box with fodder for the beast." He winked at her, saucy and rude. Victoria snapped her mouth shut and looked away. What was it she ever saw in the man?

"Please say you will come and listen to my poor attempt to educate and illuminate the masses." He seemed to sober just then and leaned forward to express the urgency of his invitation, his face filling the window. "I would be very flattered if you would deign to attend."

"I..." She retreated into the shadows. "I really don't have time for..." she unfurled the paper in her fist to wave in his direction. "I have so much to...."

The second item on the list caught her. She spared a moment to read it.

Try something new.

Blast Adeline Porter and her meddlesome ways.

How did she *know*?

"Well, I don't...."

"Lady Allington." Harold stepped away from the coach and performed one of the most elaborate and deep bows a gentleman ever attempted. It came close to mocking but fell short of being rude. He wasn't making fun of her but of himself. "I would consider the last twenty-five years in the far Continent well worth the adventure if you were there to hear of my exploits."

"Twenty-five years?" It sounded like so much longer ago than it felt. She would have sworn to God and all His ministers that it had been a year, perhaps two, since she had danced with the exciting young Harold Livingstone. No more than five when they had snuck out to watch the stars wheeling overhead in their slow dances. When she had promised she would love no other.

Such was the folly of youth. There was more than just a quarter-century between them. There were Continents, children, marriages, duties. Good heavens, put like that, was it any wonder the whole of the twenty-five years seemed to settle in on her like a great heavy blanket? Too much time had passed; too much had happened in the interim.

Try something new.

She took the time to fold the paper and slip it quietly into her reticule. She nodded, though she could not bear to take her eyes from the comforting upholstery of her carriage and into the glare of the light where Harold stood, awaiting her reply.

"Very well," she conceded and even tried to smile. "But not the horse."

Harold's grin was suddenly warmer, kinder. The way it lit his eyes warmed her too when she dared to look up. This was the young man she remembered from her youth, standing in an old man's suit and with an old man's beard. It was his eyes that told the true story of who he was.

"Wonderful. I look forward to seeing you again. My Lady."

She sat perfectly still, not looking up from the seat facing her until she was sure he was long out of earshot. When he climbed back into the driver's seat, she said as quietly as she could, "Victoria. Like you used to call me." He couldn't hear her. She made sure of that. But she had to voice the words as though keeping them inside may become a painful reminder that would someday overwhelm her.

She allowed herself a moment to remember, to marvel at his return, to wonder. In the end, speculation was pointless, though. She shook herself and wondered what she had just agreed to.

So far, Lady Porter's advice had not proven to be advantageous.

CHAPTER 5

The Deadliest Snake
Known to Man

The box reserved for her was admittedly excellent. It was large enough for eight, more than adequate for her and her companion. Thus far, Vanessa Hargraves had proven well-versed in manners and comportment, especially for one so young. But he seemed overawed by everything she saw. It had been Prunella's suggestion to hire a companion. Victoria suspected her daughters had arranged the introduction out of duty, though she was pleased they had encouraged it.

At least Vanessa never seemed to be offended by any of Victoria's comments. In fact, she often tried to hide a smile at some caustic remark made at another's expense. On the rare occasion the Dowager Countess aimed her sharp tongue at her, Vanessa seemed to absorb the words without allowing them to stir her emotions unduly. This alone was an invaluable trait that others around her should adopt as well.

However, Victoria was still unsure that she wanted to be saddled with a companion. While it was occasionally handy to have someone there as an escort, there were scant enough reasons to *need* a companion at all. In the meantime, there was little enough time alone or with Lady Porter. Vanessa was starting to seem less a companion than she was a minder to ensure that Victoria didn't embarrass her family.

She wondered whom Vanessa reported to.

It was an unworthy thought. Certainly, Prunella had her mother's best interests at heart. But there were times when it would have been relaxing to be alone with one's thoughts.

Currently, the girl was perched on the edge of a chair, overlooking the stage where Lord Livingstone was holding court to a rapt audience. The man was charismatic, to say the least. And when he laughed, which was often, the entire audience was caught up in the great humour of the man and laughed with him.

He produced a stuffed and mounted snake, a nasty, evil-looking creation with a flared neck behind a rounded head with fangs that Vanessa swore would haunt her dreams for many nights to come.

"The king cobra," Livingstone's booming voice echoed off the far walls. It was as frightening as the thought of that snake moving around alive and hungry. "Perhaps the deadliest snake known to man, it can be found in the lusher areas of the subcontinent. They are often found in trees, so the wary traveller would never see it before it dropped from a branch and onto its prey."

Vanessa shivered at the thought, but Victoria could see the delighted smile on the girl's face. Her young head was filled with adventure and exotic peoples in far off lands.

The Dowager Countess snorted and rolled her eyes. *Adventure* was simply another way to say inconvenience.

"Have you ever been, your Grace?" Vanessa's eyes lit at the idea, "to India, I mean."

"Certainly not!" Victoria huffed, insulted that she should be asked.

"I first encountered this devil upon my arrival in the Continent," Livingstone was saying. "I found the blighter in my cot on the third night. I had arrived after a blistering march with the army, and we were bivouacked on..."

The Dowager Countess soon forgot the presence of her companion, indeed of the audience in general, and found herself focused on the man on the stage. He seemed to pull all eyes to him. He was dynamic and personable, and extremely well-travelled.

Eventually, the lecture became less and less of India and more about Lord Livingstone. Yet he spoke skilfully, and the talk never became an egocentric lecture, as it might have from a lesser man. Instead, every talking point about his life was a milestone, a touchpoint to recent history that reflected the history of His Majesty's holdings in the East. In its own way, the whole talk was really quite brilliant in its design and intent.

To think, he had been sent to India as a young Captain. Major Fitzsimmons came to mind, and Victoria squashed that thought before it interfered with the lecture. Livingstone had acquitted himself well, retiring as a General in His Majesty's service. He had made several key investments mentioned in the lecture to illustrate, not his business acumen, but rather to show the progression of industry and imports between Great Briton and the East.

He made no mention of his own assets, but clearly the man had vastly increased his family's fortunes during his time abroad.

When he detailed his meeting and marrying an Englishwoman, Victoria found herself strangely affected. And when he told of this fine Lady's subsequent passing some five years ago, there was not a single dry eye in the house. Vanessa was openly weeping, poor thing, and even the Dowager Countess had to hold a tight rein on her emotions.

Yet, he wove the tale masterfully and had the audience in an uproar, laughing hard through their tears and marvelling at the treasures he had brought back with him. He had an artist recreate a drawing of an elephant, life-sized, that drew as many gasps as the cobra had. He lovingly spoke of his life abroad and the majestic beauty of the land; the Dowager Countess wondered if the man had ever truly held her as his first love or if, indeed, his first love was India itself.

At the end of his lecture, which Victoria could have sworn was only a moment after it began, the theatre erupted into a loud round of applause. Though the man was eccentric, he had captivated them for the entirety of his speech.

For his part, he seemed to draw strength from his listeners, becoming larger and larger until the stage could no longer contain him. Surely, he was as big as an elephant, as big as India. He was the world itself. His booming laughter filled the theatre with contagious mirth.

But that was the way Harold had always been. She remembered now. She remembered a great many things now.

CHAPTER 6

May I Call Upon You?

"Can you imagine?" Vanessa gushed, as they gathered their things, and the crowds filtered out. "Oh, he makes India sound so adventuresome and wonderful. Thank you, Ma'am, for taking me tonight. It was quite thrilling."

"I am glad you enjoyed it," Victoria responded, leaning so that Vanessa might appropriately position her cloak, "but we are both guests tonight. This was not my idea, so I could hardly take credit."

"May I ask, Lady Allington, who our host was? No one joined us in the box."

"That is because our host was busy. He was the one on the stage you spent the night staring at in such an interested manner."

"You know Lord Livingstone, my Lady?" The girl was positively giddy. Harold had certainly won a victory with her that day.

"I do indeed." The Dowager Countess peered over the edge of the box and saw the slow progress of the crowds as they wended their way out of the hall. It was going to be a wait. Talking was as good of a way to pass the time as any. Besides, it might be a good way to work through some of the memories she had been having since Harold came back into her life.

"I had once thought to marry him." She spoke the words just to see the girl's reaction, and she wasn't disappointed. Somehow, the Dowager

Countess had risen in the girl's estimation, though why that should have mattered, she couldn't have said.

"*Marry?*" Vanessa turned to the dark stage and the drawing of the elephant. The stage seemed to have lost some life as though it was an empty shell now, devoid of the spark that it once held. That was the problem with Harold, though. When he was not around, life seemed diminished somehow, as though he took the light from the room with him when he left. "Then you might have journeyed with him to India."

"Oh, yes. I suppose I might have." Victoria judged the movement of the thinning crowd. "Perhaps it was a good thing I listened to my mother then, wasn't it?"

Vanessa frowned. "I do not understand, my Lady."

"It is the cost of being a wife that a woman will abandon her home and family and follow a husband to the ends of the earth."

"I think it sounds exciting."

Victoria did not reply to the girl. What was there to say? Hardships always sound romantic when one is well-fed and comfortable. It is quite different when your belly is empty and there is no roof over your head.

The crowd had thinned enough that there should be little issue getting through the lobby unscathed. She turned and opened the door to the box, but there on the other side, as though he had been waiting, stood the object of their speculation. Livingstone stood with one fist raised, apparently about to knock.

"Lord Livingstone!" Vanessa spoke before she could even be properly introduced. The Dowager Countess gave her a sharp look. She would have to discuss this with the girl later when they were alone. Such a faux pas could not be ignored.

But for now, the damage was done, and Vanessa had not stopped in her ebullience. "A great honour. I was very enamoured of your speech, Sir." Vanessa sketched a deep curtsy. Her face lit up as though she had suddenly come into the presence of a god.

"Eh?" Harold Livingstone turned, only just registering that the girl was there. "Oh, thank you." His gaze was on Victoria, his hands reaching out for hers. She stepped backwards and smoothed her skirts, giving her hands some occupation.

"And you, my Lady, did you enjoy the talk as much as your friend?"

"My Lord," the Dowager Countess found her mental footing and stopped her hands, forcing them to lay still at her side. "I doubt that many have enjoyed it as much as my companion."

"It was not to your liking then?"

"On the contrary, I found it to be quite fascinating if only as a cautionary tale. I believe that it proves beyond a doubt that one must never leave London."

Lord Livingstone laughed, but he let his hands drop to his sides. "I would hate to think I convinced anyone of *that*. Surely you have travelled extensively. I vividly recall travel being one of those desires you held so closely."

"That was a long time ago, as you pointed out. The late Duke of Sunningdale was not a man predisposed to travel."

"And a wife must stay by her husband," Vanessa said with a small smile. The Dowager Countess started. She had quite forgotten the girl was there, to tell the truth. And to hear her own words back at her. Vanessa was either going to the best thing that happened or the worst. Victoria couldn't decide.

"I have spent two and a half decades in India," Livingstone waved off her assertions. "Having arrived, I chose to stay. It might be inferred that I chose not to travel at all. Once there and once back is hardly the life of a vagabond, would you not agree?"

She could not completely suppress a smile at his protestation. "You have, twice in your lifetime, journeyed halfway across the world. That makes for a full rotation, regardless of the time required. I would say you have earned the right to call yourself a traveller."

He beamed at her as though she had just said the most gracious thing he had ever heard. She thought about the last time she had seen that smile. It had been before he left for the army, before she had to tell him her mother refused to allow him to court her. Before she had said goodbye.

She never let him know, about how much she had wept that night. The tears torn from her, painful, excruciating, a piece of her had died. In the morning, she buried her youth and followed her mother to the Estate of a wealthy Duke.

Silly bit of a girl. The Duke gave her title, money, and children. He had been a good man in his own way: sturdy, reliable, dependable.

As for the girl who wept for something she couldn't have, well, the young are often foolish. Vanessa was proof enough of that. She looked as though she would be packed and on her way in a steamship within an hour, given half a chance.

There had been a time and a place for youthful enthusiasm. But that was a long time ago. She had little use or energy for such things now.

"Lady Allington," Livingstone cocked his head to one side as he watched her think through all these things. "I...formally...request permission to call upon you later this week."

Vanessa gasped. Lady Allington found herself bereft of speech. It was ridiculous. Mad.

"You may."

She didn't recognise the voice that answered, though it came from her mouth. She wondered if this could be placed under the edict of 'try something new.'

"Excellent!" Harold's delighted response could have been heard back in India.

CHAPTER 7

Dance Like No One is Watching

The day Lord Livingstone came to call, Victoria made it quite clear that he must follow certain rules to court her. First, he was forbidden to drive any conveyance they rode in together. He'd been reckless as a boy and had not proven more prudent with age. "Besides," she admonished him, "you have a perfectly good driver whom you are paying to ride beside you."

He only shrugged at this, taking it as a suggestion and not so much as the edict she had intended. "There is nothing so thrilling as holding the reins." Her reaction must have been telling because he immediately backed down and raised his hands in surrender. "As the Lady wishes, of course. I shall content myself with the thrill of your presence."

We shall see about that. She gathered her wrap as the air was getting chillier and the phaeton was open to the elements. She preferred her coach, but it was better to be open to view for decency's sake. Of course, that meant tongues would wag, but such was inevitable once he returned to London. There weren't many who remembered that he and she had once been considered star-crossed lovers, as it were. But there were a few, and gossip to the Ton was lamp oil to a struck match.

The Dowager Countess told herself she did not mind the chatter behind her back when the topic was regarding her and the retired General. He was entertaining, and despite his boisterous nature, he was the perfect gentleman. His time in the wilds of India had not turned him into a heathen.

He was no less of a gentleman than he had been as a young pup. It was the same character that filled the stage, that held the attention of the gentry at his fingertips and balanced the full span of the Ton upon his every word. He was simply larger than life and unashamed of his love of all things.

Thus, it was understandable, even expected that close associations with the man would draw out the girl in her.

They took a turn around the park one particularly crisp morning. The driver easing the hose around bumps and holes with enviable skill, and Victoria caught the open looks of interest. People stumbled and stopped abruptly to see her being so openly courted. Though there were a few smiles, and no disapproving looks that she could see, the universal reaction of pure shock made her wonder what it was that was so surprising.

"Should I be embarrassed that I have not yet passed away?" she asked in frustration after the sixth such occurrence.

"What was that?" Harold leaned over to hear her better. She hadn't realised she had spoken aloud, though apparently not loudly enough. "Look at that." She nodded at a mother and daughter who had stopped, packages in hands to watch the phaeton go past. "They gape and gasp as if I carried a dead fish in the cart."

Harold turned towards the two in question and waved to them.

"Stop that." Victoria scolded but couldn't completely suppress a surprised laugh.

"I should point out, I suppose," he said in that slow way that preceded his sense of humour, "that this 'cart' belongs to me and is currently driven by my man."

"And I thank God for his service."

"So," Harold continued, the light of mirth in his eyes, "that would make you the fish." His grin split his beard, and even white teeth showed like a beacon. The Dowager Countess huffed and refused to meet his eyes. The truth was, she had no wish to encourage his impertinence but could not face him directly, lest she begin laughing. It seemed, however, that her efforts were wasted, for he seemed to know the effect he had on her and chuckled.

Rather put out, she ignored him for several minutes until he started asking her questions about the life she had after he left. He wanted to know about her children and even about her late husband. He listened attentively and respectfully when she spoke of his rival, to her surprise. She began answering him with her caustic wit and bitterness. Still, he kept gently rephrasing her stories until they sounded silly and charming. Soon she found herself not only indulging his quips but embellishing her stories herself just to illicit his laughter.

Several days later, Harold escorted her to a concert at the same hall where he had enthralled the Ton. The strains of *The Magic Flute* echoed through the hall. Victoria found herself in the same box with Vanessa once more. This time, the girl had a slightly less advantageous view as she sat behind Lord Livingstone. He contentedly watched Victoria more often than he did the musicians.

Though it was off-season for the grand balls, there were a few who desperately tried to get one more in before their Christmas travels. The stir caused by Harold and Victoria was fanned into even greater flames when they arrived together.

As for Livingstone, he seemed immune to gossip. In fact, he appeared rather proud that her name was linked to his. When they danced, his eyes were focused on her, and she discovered she had no idea who else attended the ball.

His attentiveness was indeed charming. He even led Victoria to the edge of the dance floor. Her face was flushed, and she was breathing hard after a rather energetic turn. He bowed low and offered to fetch her some punch, and she retired to the windows to catch her breath.

The bower where he had placed her was quite congenial. She settled in the chair nearest the window. She ran her fingers down the curtains, exploring the thickness and quality of the material. Absolutely delightful. She considered whether she ought to arrange for a similar window covering at the Dower House and mentally made several notes to that effect.

A voice nearby caught her ear. "Absolutely ridiculous."

"Shameful. At their age," another answered.

Victoria allowed the curtain to fall. Two women were on the other side of the table from her and had their backs to her.

"His behaviour might be excused, being in the uncivilised country for so long, the poor dear, but *her*?"

"Prancing around like a schoolgirl," the first woman lamented, "how embarrassing."

The blood drained from Victoria's face.

It was time to go home. She spun on one heel and nearly tripped over Adeline.

"My dear!" The woman was nearly aglow. The two matrons who had been talking vanished as soon as they saw who was standing there. "How lovely it is to see you dancing and enjoying yourself. I am delighted to see the changes you have...."

"Changes?" Victoria spat the word. It was all she could do to keep the volume down, but the vitriol would not stay out of her mouth. "Changes? You've played me for a fool. You both have!" She shot the last to Harold, who had returned with two glasses of punch and a confused look on his face.

The Dowager Countess gathered her tattered dignity and stormed from the ballroom, ignoring the calls from both friend and suitor. It was time to act her age. As for her children, well, they could take their mother as she was. It was too late to change now, and frankly, that was too great a sacrifice, even for them.

She fled to the shadows of the coach and sent the driver back for his master. Before retiring, she called for Vanessa. It was time the girl earned her salary.

CHAPTER 8

When in Doubt, Flee

V anessa hovered about nervously as Victoria issued orders with an experienced eye to what needed doing. The Dowager Countess set the girl packing for the Dower House. The children would likely not miss her. She had no intention of remaining in London and be a laughingstock for the *Ton's* wagging tongues.

The *Ton* was more lenient with Harold because he was a wealthy gentleman. But even he had been the object of those vipers' sharp tongues.

She had made a fool of herself, that much was evident. But even fools were forgotten when the next object of ridicule came along. As a Dowager, she wasn't expected to partake in the Season. Better to be forgotten in the country where she belonged.

As her companion saw to the bags and the carriage, Victoria held her stomach and tried to calm herself. She'd had little sleep the night before. The darkness had echoed voices from her memories. The matrons from the ball and their false pity haunted even her waking hours. But their mocking blended with an older, more bitter voice from a distant past.

Once in the carriage, she informed Vanessa, in no uncertain terms, that she was not to speak unless quite necessary. Even the driver seemed muted and made heavy efforts to avoid holes and ruts that seemed to be his favourite targets.

"The boy is a fool. A dreamer. Mind you, he will lose his family's fortune in no time." Her mother's voice rattled with the carriage wheels and pounded her ears with every hoof falling on the dirt roads.

"You *will* marry a man with stability, someone with the means to care for you and your children, not some will-o-the-wisp who flits from one thing to another."

Mile by mile, the memory of how her youth and...well, what she had once considered love was flayed by her mother's sharp tongue. She had never been so cruel to her own children. She had attempted to guide them in a better life, but she had not *prohibited* them from their marriages, had she? Both of her daughters had made move matches. Unlike her, they had not married for position or wealth. It gave her shallow comfort as the day progressed.

If they had heard the gossip, they had not let on. Victoria hardly ever saw them. She had arrived at Sunningdale a week ago, and not once had they managed to dine together as a family. Frederick had assured her they would once the Season paused for the Holiday. They would have to dine without her.

She was sorry she would miss seeing Henry. Perhaps the boy would visit her in the country before returning to France.

This was the second time she had walked away from Harold, the second time she had left the man who made her feel light and free. Only this time, instead of her mother's voice, she heard the gossip of meddling old women. This time, she could blame no one but herself.

She had not walked away from love. She had *run*.

Love. The word felt strange on her tongue. All three of her married children were in love with their spouses. It hadn't been like that for her and John. They had done their duty and learned to appreciate one another.

Now John was gone, and so was their home. She had been given a second chance at love, but she had run from it.

Harold was in London. She had left him there.

When she arrived, Victoria had felt a moment of remorse and penned a letter to Adeline. When she called Vanessa to have it dispatched, the girl informed her that Lady Porter had a message. It seemed the old friends had had the same idea. Vanessa held out a small silver tray bearing a crisp white envelope with Adeline's familiar scrawl.

c/o The Dowager Countess of Sunningdale

My dearest, oldest, and most wonderful friend.

I said I missed the girl you once were. And I suppose that it might have been myself I missed. I, too, was carefree once. You and I seemed to be so much alike. Perhaps I pushed you too hard to be something you once were and no longer are.

Please accept my sincerest apologies. Please. I have known and treasured our friendship for so many years. I could not bear it if that were to be taken from me.

I would like to explain my reasoning for embarking on this journey. I do not excuse any offence, but please hear me out.

Speak with Kindness: Kindness begets kindness. When you speak from kindness, you become more kind to others, yes, but most importantly, to yourself. I know of no one who deserves kindness more than my old friend. I only wanted you to be kinder to yourself because you are deserving of love.

Try Something New: New things challenge the mind and keep the soul from wilting under the weight of boredom. New also illuminates aspects of ourselves we might not even recognise.

Enjoy the Moment: Life is fleeting. It should never be squandered in self-recrimination or regret. Allow the past to remain in the past. You cannot live there. You are now with your family, surrounded by your loved ones. Let go of all else.

Look on the Bright Side: There is always a bright side. You were younger, freer than I have seen you in many years in the past weeks. Whatever happened to make you run, look to the enjoyment you had, and treasure those moments.

Finally, Laugh More: You have the most wonderful laugh. Infectious and melodic. I miss that more than anything else. Perhaps it was unfair of me to attempt to have that in my life again, but I pray there is laughter in yours. It is my fervent hope that you find joy again in that laughter.

More than anything else, I pray that you find love again, my dearest friend.

If you would care to know, incidentally, no one has seen Lord Living-stone since the ball.

Remember, my dear, look on the bright side.

Your dear friend in all things.

Adeline.

The Dowager Countess lay the paper on the table before her and stared out of the window.

No regrets? Of course, everyone had regrets. Twenty-five years of regrets. Her mother had assured her that, in time, she would learn to love her husband. And for twenty-five years, she assumed that keeping his house and having his children, well, these things were love, were they not?

He had been a good man. He had been good to her. But had he been good *for* her? What would life have been like with Harold? What grand adventures, what impetuousness would her life have been?

No Regrets?

"I should have told you, Harold. A quarter of a century ago and four days ago. "I love you. I always have. I should have told you."

She dropped her head in her hands and let the tears flow. It was a gentle weeping, silent and as much a release as it was sorrow.

She didn't see Vanessa slip quietly from the room.

CHAPTER 9

Fetch the Preacher

On Christmas Eve, Victoria had only just settled in her sitting room with a book and a cup of tea when Vanessa informed her that she had a visitor.

"Who is it?" she asked. She had no acquaintances in the country. Perhaps the Pastor was making his Christmas rounds.

Then, a surge of hope was born within her. "Is it Henry?"

Vanessa looked down in dismay.

"No, my Lady. It is Lord Livingstone," she said and fled from the room.

"Vanessa," Victoria hissed but the girl had gone, and she couldn't very well shout with a guest in the house.

Victoria barely had time to compose herself that Harold was at the door.

"Lady Allington, how lovely you look in the glow of the morning sun," he said as he bowed and presented her with a tantalizing box of sweets.

"Thank you, Lord Livingstone. May I offer you some refreshment?" she asked politely, placing the sweets on the table.

When he refused, she asked, "What brings you to the country, my Lord?"

"Surely you know," he said, his eyes searching her face. She did not maintain eye contact and merely shrugged. She dared to hope that he meant that he was here for her, but she needed him to come out and say it. She had been humiliated enough.

"A new horse, perhaps? Or are you trading spices with the local farmers?"

"Victoria," he began but at her stony glare, he corrected himself. "Lady Allington, have I said or done anything to offend you?"

"No, of course not. Why do ask?" she said, brushing invisible dust from her gown.

"You left London so abruptly. And you left no word," he said, his voice trailing off.

"Did we have plans that I have forgotten about?" she asked. "If so, I do apologize for my lack of manners."

"No plans as such. But an understanding...I thought," he said.

"How do you mean?" she said.

"I was under the impression that I was courting you these last few days," he said.

"How absurd! I am much too old to be courted," she said, waving it off with a smile.

Lord Livingstone looked deeply affronted. He almost shouted his reply, "If I am not too old to court you, then you are not too old to be courted."

Victoria was so shocked she finally looked at his face. When their eyes met, her heart melted a little at the passion she saw on his face.

Harold approached and kneeled before her.

"My dearest Victoria, surely you know that I love you!" he said. His eyes bore into hers. When he reached for her hand, she let him take it.

"I have always loved you," he said, his voice cracking with emotion. He placed a kiss on her hand and rested his forehead on it before releasing it.

Victoria was struck dumb. Her every hope, her every dream was within her grasp, and she couldn't say a word.

Harold rose a pleading look in his eyes.

"I had hoped you felt the same way. We had such fun together this week, taking rides, and dancing. It felt like old times. But I see I've been an old fool," he said.

He bowed and made to leave. "I thank you for your hospitality and I apologize if I have inconvenienced you in any way."

He made it to the door of the sitting room before Victoria found her voice.

"Stop!" she yelled, standing abruptly, and rushing to him like he was a train she didn't want to miss.

"Don't go," she said, and he paused by the door without turning.

She searched breathlessly for the words, for something witty or clever to say. But all she could voice were raw emotions.

"I love you, Harold."

He turned slowly, a tentative smile on his lips.

"I'm sorry, Lady Allington. My hearing isn't what it used to be," he said with a twinkle in his eye.

Victoria laughed. "Come here and kiss me you old fool," she said.

He heard *that* well enough. In less than two strides he was upon her. Victoria felt as breathless as a maid. He took her by the shoulders and kissed her gently. He pulled back and looked at her face, his giddy grin matching her own. She wrapped her arms around his neck and pulled him down for another, longer kiss. This one lasted much longer. In fact, they were still kissing when Vanessa came in to announce another visitor.

They pulled apart reluctantly and Victoria asked who had come calling, "Is it the Preacher?"

"No, my Lady," she said with a smile. "Your sons are here."

When Frederick and Henry entered the sitting room, they seemed surprised to find Lord Livingstone in attendance.

They were even more surprised when their mother rushed to them and embraced them in turn.

"Mother, are you ill? Is that why you left without leaving word?" asked Frederick.

Victoria was so pleased to see her sons that she forgot why she had been so cross with her children in the first place. Now that she had been reminded, her eyes narrowed as she sat on the divan.

"I left two days ago, have you only now realised I had gone?" she said with more bitterness than she felt. It was a habit she needed to break.

"No, of course not. It's only that Josephina's family arrived yesterday, and I had to see to my guests. We've come to fetch you home," he said.

Home.

"This is my home now," she said, waving at the room in general.

"Mother, it is Christmas. We should spend the Holiday as a family," Henry said, coming to sit next to his mother. "I've missed you and there's so much I want to tell you," he said earnestly.

"Have you really? I thought you stayed in France with your sister so you could be rid of me," she said with a sniff.

Frederick came to sit on her other side. He took his mother's hand. "I'm sorry if we've neglected you these last few days. It wasn't our intention," he said.

"Your sisters and your wife can't possibly want me to come back. They've made it abundantly clear that my presence is merely tolerated out of obligation," she said, her back stiff, looking ahead.

"It's true that, in the past, you were somewhat rigid and unforgiving. One would say you were overly critical, especially with Prunella and Arabella. But everyone has noticed how much you have changed recently. For the better, I might add," said Frederick.

The words, though true and spoken gently, were hard for her to hear.

Harold had moved away to stand near the window to give them some privacy, but he had heard every word. More than once, he wanted to charge to Victoria's defence. But it seemed this airing out of grievances was necessary for them to move on.

He cleared his throat.

"Hello, I am Lord Livingstone," he said extending a hand to Frederick.

"I am Frederick Allington, Duke of Sunningdale. I believe we met briefly at a ball last week. You are acquainted with Major Fitzsimmons, I believe?"

"Only in passing," said Harold. "I am a personal acquaintance of Lady Allington."

At this, Henry rose and introduced himself.

"How are you acquainted with my Mother, Sir," Henry asked, his eyes assessing the older man.

"I was once one of her suitors. And, if she'll have me, I hope to make her my wife as soon as it can be arranged," he said, winking at Victoria.

Victoria giggled and replied," Of course, I'll marry you. Where is that Preacher when you need him?"

Frederick and Henry could only stare open-mouthed as their mother rose from the divan, strode to Lord Livingstone, and planted a kiss on his lips.

Epilogue

It had been the best Christmas Victoria had ever remembered having. While she and her sons were talking, Vanessa had packed their things and closed the Dower House. When Frederick asked his mother to return to London with them, Harold had intervened and said he would bring their mother.

Vanessa was at a loss as to which carriage she should board. The proper thing would have been to follow Lady Allington, but Lord Livingstone was adamant that, as they were now betrothed, it was entirely acceptable for the couple to ride in a carriage together. In the end, she rode with the Duke and his brother.

Prunella was the first to notice the change in Victoria, but Arabella soon came around and cautiously allowed her mother to be closer. She was skittish, but when she found that her mother was no longer angry or bitter, she absorbed her mother's attention like desert sands drinking water. In contrast, Frederick was on board with the "new her" almost immediately. But then he had always been the most forgiving of them all, even with the whole matter of the dual behind him.

As the second son, and a boy of only fourteen, Henry hadn't been subjected to as much of his mother's severity as the others. He had mostly been ignored altogether and so he too was grateful for the attention she was lavishing on him. Beyond that, the boy was happy to spend time with the Barrington twins, Sophia and Jackson.

As for Major Fitzsimmons and Viscount Pommeray, they had no opinion one way or another; if their wives were happy, they were happy.

Josephina, Frederick's wife, was more than happy to embrace the new Victoria. Especially as she blessed her mother-in-law with the greatest of gifts: her first grandchild would be born in late Spring. Victoria was overjoyed with the news.

To celebrate the new addition to the family, Prunella announced they should hold a ball on New Year's Eve.

"That's only a few days away," Victoria gasped. "There's no time to...." The look on Prunella's face stopped her mid-sentence. Arabella was already pouting. "No time to waste. Let's begin planning at once."

Arabella's expression lit up the room, and Prunella spontaneously hugged her mother. Victoria was becoming fond of such displays of affection. Truthfully, it was likely that such a small warning would mean a small crowd. But she reminded herself sternly that enjoying those who *did* arrive was certainly better than lamenting those who did not.

She and Lady Barrington, Josephina's mother, helped with the preparations. It seemed that she was not alone in having to rein herself in from taking over. While *Enjoying the Moment* was still new to her, she had to adjust, as she learned new ways to let go. To that end, she gave up altogether and let the younger generation handle the ball while she nurtured a budding new friendship with Lady Barrington. They had so much in common.

As New Year's Eve approached, she found the ball coming together nicely and was quite proud of her daughters' accomplishments. She made sure to tell them often.

Adeline was right. Kindness begets kindness. Victoria felt as though a great knot in her chest had been untied, one she had not even realised was there. Of course, her dear friend was coming to the ball. She had replied to the invitation with enthusiasm. Harold would be there, of course. He had come calling every day and made her promise they would be wed as soon as possible. She had no objections, but she wanted to enjoy her family and the Holiday. He understood completely.

The musicians had only just begun playing when the first guests arrived. Adeline was rendered speechless when Victoria embraced her and grabbed her hands. "There you are." She whispered with a certain wonder in her voice. "My dearest friend. I have awaited your return."

Victoria tried to respond over a sudden lump in her throat but found herself suddenly whisked onto the dance floor by the handsome Lord Livingstone.

She started and then began laughing. "I didn't see you come in, you startled me."

That booming laugh she feared she would never hear again filled her ears and soothed her soul. I had a thing or two to discuss with Frederick before the ball," Harold said cryptically before reaching around her waist, and for a moment, she found herself waltzing.

Scandalous. Indecent. Wonderful.

"Mother." Prunella hissed as they bowed to the centre and wended their way to the edge of the ballroom. "That dancing..."

"Prunella, dear," said Victoria taking Harold's hand. There's no scandal if one is engaged." Prunella burst out laughing and ran to Arabella, presumably to tell her what their mother had just said, for Arabella started laughing as well.

Victoria laughed too, and Harold beamed at his beloved.

"At our age, there's no time to waste. Besides, I understand India is lovely this time of year." She looked into the eyes of her love. "How soon might we leave?"

The End

Friends with The Lady

THE LADY SERIES BOOK SIX

Prologue

L ord and Lady Barrington welcomed their twins on a windy March day. A day filled with cold but crisp sunlight. It was almost Spring, and flowers were seen blooming in every nook and cranny in Brighton, a town well-known for its exotic floral displays.

Excitement prevailed, as friends and neighbours heard about the news of the twins' safe delivery. They rejoiced at their mother's health, as delivering twins at her advanced age was always risky, even with the best physicians.

Indeed, the pregnancy had come as a shock to the entire family. Never more so than Lady Barrington, who believed her family was complete eight years ago when Clarissa was born. After a few moments of chagrin at the thought of the physical discomforts of the months ahead, she had announced the happy news to Lord Barrington.

"Perhaps it'll be a boy!" he replied with great excitement. The first three children had been girls, and Lord Barrington despaired at the idea of having to leave his fortune to his feckless nephew Bartholomew.

As it turned out, Lord and Lady Barrington were blessed with both a boy and a girl: Jackson and Sophia. Their siblings, Camilla, Josephina, and Clarissa were overjoyed. The twins were live dolls to them, and they enjoyed helping the nurse care for the little angels.

Soon, there was a flurry of activity to find the best governess and tutors for the twins' most refined upbringing and education. Many great minds applied for this prominent position, asking to play their part in the twins' upbringing; Lord Barrington was one of the wealthiest landowners in the area.

Time passed. As their sisters married and left home, the twins missed them terribly. Lord and Lady Barrington had their occupations. They expected their youngest children to be content with their studies and with each other.

One day, during Josephina's Season in London, Jackson met Henry Allington while enjoying a family outing in the park. They became fast friends. When Henry asked for his help in dealing with a scoundrel, Jackson did not hesitate to offer it.

Jackson solicited Josephina's assistance as the matter was financial, and he had no money. She was his favourite sister, and if someone could come up with a scheme, it was Josephina. As she had spent all of her pin money, she proposed to discuss the matter discretely with Henry's brother, the Earl of Sunningdale. Arabella, her best friend, who happened to be one of Henry's sisters, had only recently been introduced.

Not only had the scheme worked, but not a month later, Josephina had married Frederick Allington, the Earl of Sunningdale. As soon as they were settled in their married life, Josephina sent for her siblings as often as Lord and Lady Barrington were willing to part with them, which was quite often.

As for Henry, he and Arabella also made frequent visits to Sunningdale Manor. They soon became thick as thieves and were inseparable until Henry left England to travel to France. What started as a holiday became a permanent arrangement. He decided to stay in Paris indefinitely with his eldest sister Prunella and Captain George Fitzsimmons.

As Henry had always loved the sea, Sophia and Jackson couldn't begrudge their friend's choice. The Captain had taken him under his wing and filled his head with stories about a life of adventure.

CHAPTER 1

Of Twins and Tweens

The Earl of Sunningdale hosted a New Year's Eve ball to celebrate his first heir's arrival, though the child wouldn't be born until the following Spring. It was a last-minute decision, and the ladies of the house had scrambled to put the ball together in haste. In truth, even if no one but family attended the ball, it would be a delightful event.

Nonetheless, the Ton quickly accepted their invitations and descended upon Sunningdale Manor in droves. Jackson, Sophia, and Henry could not attend the ball, as they were not out yet, being only fourteen and fifteen respectively, and were left to their own devices.

Unsupervised, the young people made their entertainment: finding several games to play to pass the time, including chasing each other around the grounds upon horseback, working out complex raids of the kitchens, and perusing the most forbidden books in Sunningdale's extensive library.

On the night of the ball itself, the trio was especially put out, feeling as though they were being treated too much like children, when in truth, they were nearly grown. In utter defiance, they set out to prove how childish they could be. They made a fort out of sheets and brooms in the nursery and filled it with cushions and blankets. Jackson, who dreamed of travelling the world, took them on a make-believe adventure to India, a game which turned out to be more amusing than any of them had anticipated and kept them occupied most of the evening.

When the clock struck midnight, Henry produced a half-filled bottle of Champagne he'd pilfered from an unattended tray, along with three glasses. They toasted the New Year and made solemn vows always to be friends.

Sophia suggested they put something more tangible behind such a promise and added that they should send letters to stay in touch.

The boys groaned at her suggestion, but the steely look she gave them had them nodding in agreement.

"The letters do not have to be formal. We are hardly writing to the Queen," said Sophia. "And I see no reason for them to be very long. I am quite sure you lot can string a few words together to tell us what is going on in your life. At the very least, each of you could inform the others where you are in the world from time to time."

"Very well," replied Henry. He would have to write to his mother and sisters anyhow. What were a few more letters when daily correspondence already made up a portion of his day?

"I fear you are right, Sophia. You and I will be apart for the first time, and I shall miss you," mumbled Jackson, his voice low.

Sophia grabbed each of their hands, pulling them in for an impulsive hug. Her cheeks flushed with excitement.

"We should save all the letters in a box," Sophia added. "Then one day, when we are old and grey, we can open them and recall every one of our memories." Her eyes sparkled with excitement.

"You have captured my imagination, Sophia. It will be wonderful to hear from each of you while I am away in France," said Henry with a smile.

After committing to the plan, they brought forward their hands, stuck them together, and shook on it, the way they had seen the adults do when settling matters of honour. At this point, they were interrupted by Henry's mother, the Dowager Countess.

"It is after three in the morning! Why has no one sent you to bed?" she asked with a reproving tone.

"Dearest Mama, I am no longer a child. I am fifteen years old. A man my age or even younger might go to sea as a ship's boy!" Henry replied, head held high. The Dowager took one look at the makeshift tent and raised an eyebrow. As she had recently vowed to be kinder, she did not comment and merely bid them goodnight before departing.

The festive mood had died immediately upon the Dowager Countess' arrival. Though they each had their own rooms to go to, Henry, Jackson, and Sophia decided to bed down in the nursery one last time, like they had when they were children. The governess put her foot down at this. The boys would be allowed to enjoy the tent, while Sophia was sent to her bed.

Sophia felt the separation keenly and had difficulty getting to sleep. Finally, instead of staring at the ceiling all night, she began writing letters in her mind and storing them for the future. *What a very lady-like thing to do*, she thought. She was smiling under her covers, enjoying every turn of phrase. She imagined where she might be when she wrote each letter and the clever witticisms and droll observations she would use to bring a smile to each of their faces.

As far as her brother Jackson was concerned, he had already taken the matter of the letters in stride. While he wasn't entirely as enthralled with the idea the way Henry and Sophia were, he was not wholly opposed to it either, if anyone chose to follow through. In all likelihood, they would develop another scheme on the morrow as they often did, which would displace this idea. But if they followed up on the letter-writing campaign, he would, of course, comply. He was nothing if not a man of his word.

Longing for the Post

S ophia was sitting on the edge of the water fountain in the extensive gardens on the Barrington Estate. Watching and listening to the water flow was both peaceful and calming. This was her favourite place to visit when she needed to escape and think about things.

Today was one of those days where she was dreamily lost in her thoughts. She was thinking about Jackson and how dreadfully she missed him now that he left for Eton. Life had changed. Jackson was at boarding school. Henry had moved to Paris, indefinitely, to live with his sister. It was just her now, and she found that very hard. Her lessons, at the hands of her governess, were quite tedious and dull.

Jackson and Henry had promised to write, but Jackson had written to her only once thus far. His letter informed her that he had reached Eton safely, settled into his lodgings, and made new friends. He also mentioned receiving a letter from Henry to say that he had settled into his new life in Paris.

Hearing this news, Sophia began expecting a letter from Henry. She'd received Jackson's most recent letter a fortnight ago. That there was still no letter from Henry in all this time left a bad taste in her mouth. Was his word worth so little?

She told herself it didn't matter. Only, the longer she waited, the more her thoughts seemed to rest on Henry. Try as she might to focus on other things, her mind kept coming back to Henry.

"Miss Barrington, you have a letter."

Miss Allen had caught her entirely off guard. Sophia had been completely lost in her own thoughts.

"You will find it inside the house." The governess nodded towards the mansion.

As soon as she heard Miss Allen's words, Sophia rushed back inside, picking up the bottom edge of her gown to run across the garden all the quicker.

"Mama, where is my letter?" Sophia breathlessly inquired once inside the house.

Her mother handed her the missive, and she immediately recognised the handwriting. Unfortunately, this particular letter wasn't from the one she hoped it would be from. It was from her brother Jackson.

She let out a sigh and dropped herself down onto a chaise longue. Though disappointment filled her heart initially, she *was* delighted to hear from her twin.

She tore open the letter and started reading. Jackson told her of his time at Eton, how he was maturing at every step, and how supportive his new friends were. At the end of the letter, he asked Sophia if she had heard from Henry.

Sophia wrote back to her brother at once. She told Jackson how much she missed him, calling to mind the long evening strolls and their rides in the countryside, last time he'd been home. She mentioned that he must buy her a necklace full of rubies for being away and needed him to teach her how to sit a galloping horse properly as soon as he came back. She also informed him that she wanted to learn how to do archery, too, as she'd heard he had become an excellent shot at Eton.

At the end of her letter, she mentioned that she hadn't heard from Henry in quite a long time, but she planned to write to him soon.

"When have I thought about that?" she whispered to herself under her breath and laughed, for she well knew how Henry was always on her mind these days.

Now that she had sealed Jackson's letter, and sent the valet to mail it, she sat and thought about writing to Henry.

She ran to her bedroom and locked the door. She wasn't sure why she was acting so strangely, but well, there was something about such a letter that called for privacy. Of course, they had made a promise. And there was nothing improper in writing to him. Besides, if Henry had no plans to keep the promise, she would jog his memory to keep it.

Sophia grabbed the folder where all her clean sheets of stationery were kept. She took out the best piece of creamy parchment, her favourite quill pen, and some black ink. She sat down at her table and wrote a letter to Henry.

She was unsure if such correspondence was seemly. They had been acting childishly when they made that foolish promise. But, well, Henry had seemed as excited as she. So, there really could be no harm in it and possibly much to gain. She began to write.

CHAPTER 3
Lines on the Front

Dear Henry,

I hope my letter finds you in the best of health.

I was just reminiscing about that New Year's Eve night where we promised to write each other letters and keep each other informed about our life events. Can you believe how fast time flies? But here I am writing to you, and I shall be eagerly awaiting your reply.

As you know, Jackson has gone to Eton, and since then, he has written to me only twice. He talked about you in both his letters. So I've decided to initiate what was to be our letter-writing tradition. Perhaps Paris has made you busy, and you are still settling in. Perhaps the training may be challenging, and you have less spare time to think about such things. Or perhaps you have forgotten our promise and all about your friend here in England already? I hope not, for I have always counted you as my dear friend.

I hope your training for the military is going perfectly well. I have always felt you would make an outstanding soldier. However, I confess to some trepidation.

I sometimes feel intimidated by the idea of you joining the army. I know that such a life contains a certain amount of peril, especially with so much unsettled in the world and the potential of being called to war so high. Of course, you were always the responsible one among the three of us.

I am sure you will fare well and undoubtedly become a brigadier or even a general one day.

Mama told me that we shall be paying fewer visits to Sunningdale Manor in the near future. Of course, there seems little to draw me back with you in Paris, though the Estate is quite beautiful. Perhaps it is for the best. To return only makes me sad, for the hall and grounds feel so empty when you are not there.

I asked her where you will be settling in Paris when you are not deployed, and she told me you should likely stay with your sister. It is good to know that there is someone to look after you in Paris and that you shall not be all alone in a strange country.

I hope all is going well for you. If not, may whatever cause you trouble become easier over time. I am saying this because I have heard the military can be a hard life. It is perhaps silly to say such things, for I know your nature is to persevere. In no time at all, I expect you will be wearing an officer's uniform. I imagine you shall look quite dashing and, I eagerly anticipate such a time when I might see you.

In the meantime, take good care of yourself, Henry. Give my regards to your dear sister, Prunella.

Your friend.

Sophia.

Henry put the letter down and closed his eyes, drinking it all in.

Sophia had actually written to him. Was this a dream? He thought she would never write him a letter because maybe she thought their idea had been so stupid. Why was his heart beating so fast, as though it was going to jump out of his chest? It was only a letter!

"What is happening to you, Henry?" murmured Henry to himself. "Get a grip, man!"

But the feeling was pleasant, albeit giddy. He took a deep breath and sat on the edge of his bed. He put the letter down carefully. Whatever was happening within him, he knew this was something new. He surely had not felt this way before.

All the time they had spent together, all those years. He had only ever thought of Sophia as his best friend, someone he could always rely on. Then, one day, the feelings changed into something else. He hadn't known how much he would miss her when he left for France.

He re-read the letter, time and time again. It was precisely the sort of letter he had wished for when he dared to dream about such things. It had not been too formal, which is more what he would expect from his childhood friend, Sophia. He had been waiting for almost a month for this letter to finally arrive. He was thinking about her with the same intensity as she was thinking of him, but he had dared not write to her, to make the first move.

The letter not only made him smile, it made him blush. He didn't know what he would write in response or when exactly he would write it. He just knew that he was so taken by the letter that he made himself late for training. He grabbed his hat from the side table and rushed out for the training practice, taking up his sword.

CHAPTER 4

News from Paris

Sophia was holding the reply letter from Henry, and her hands were trembling. There was a smile on her face, and her cheeks were red from blushing. She could smell him on the parchment. She inhaled deeply, drinking in his scent. She'd not even read it yet, but her heart was beating with excitement.

She went to Papa's study. She knew it would be spare until he returned from London, where he had gone for a few days on business. She closed the doors behind her, as though this letter were a secret. Maybe it was, of sorts. Even though she and Henry were childhood friends, there was something about this correspondence that she didn't want to share with any of her family.

She sat on Papa's study chair. Here was the long-awaited letter. The one she'd been anticipating for weeks. She unfolded the letter carefully, wondering what it might say.

Her heart pounded. Her name sounded even better when he wrote it. Gooseflesh spread all over her body.

Dear Sophia,

Thank you for writing to me. It was a delight to receive your letter.
I am very well, thank you. I trust that you are in the best of spirits too.
My training routine is demanding and rigorous, but I love it, hard

work though it is, and I am learning much. When I get back from train-ing, I feel the effects, and I require a good night's sleep before I get up at dawn for another new day to start.

I did write to your brother, Jackson, a while ago. It is good to know that he has gotten used to his surroundings at University so quickly. He has a tremendous academic mind.

Paris is beautiful, and I lodge with my sister, Prunella. She and her husband make things somewhat more manageable for me here. Her husband, Major Fitzsimmons, is my senior. You can say he is one of the few people who inspired me to join the military.

You write that you are very concerned about me. I am honoured by your concern. Rest assured, my dear Sophia, I am in the best of health, and I take good care of myself. I am enjoying the training so far.

Once again, I am glad to hear from you. It made me happy to discover I am still within your thoughts.

Sophia closed the letter for a second. Had she made him happy? Had her letter made him happy? Oh Lord, Henry was actually glad to hear from her!

She felt immense pleasure. She opened the letter and continued reading from where she had left off.

I must confess, I think about you as well. When the days are long, I think upon you and take comfort in the memories of our time together.

I must also confess; I did not write to you first because I thought perhaps you were angry or exasperated with me. So, I thought, I shall wait for your letter. And somehow, I knew you would write to me, even though I feared you would not.

Do you remember us suggesting we save all our letters in a box? Well, I have saved yours. I hope this shall be the first of many more letters, as I indeed shall write to you many more. I confess, I also keep Jackson's letters, though I keep his correspondence in a separate container altogether. I wonder if you do the same.

I am eagerly anticipating another letter from you soon that I might add it to my box.

Yours

Henry.

Sophia held the letter close to her chest and closed her eyes. She brought the parchment close to her nose to smell it again. While she could smell the ink pigment, there was also a slight scent clinging to the paper that belonged to him, she imagined. Or perhaps it was Paris itself she smelled.

She was being ridiculous. She set down the letter with a wry laugh. She was falling for her childhood friend. He was simply a boy in the military, many miles away from her. There was probably nothing but feelings of warm friendship on his side. Not...well, thoughts of love or romance.

Still laughing it off, she wandered into the parlour where her mother was reading by the fire. It was Autumn, and it had often been raining of late, so there was a distinct chill in the air.

"Come sit by the fire," said Mama. Mama's face was curious. "I noticed you were sitting in your Father's study all by yourself. Is everything all right, Sophia?"

"Yes, it was nothing, Mama. I just wanted to read a few pages alone in silence. There is nothing to be concerned about," replied Sophia.

Mama didn't look convinced, but she didn't push her daughter.

"Have you heard anything from your friend Henry? It has been quite a long time now since he moved away, and I wondered how he's getting on in France."

Shivers moved across Sophia's body, and she was quite still for a moment. Why would her mother ask such a thing? Had she been aware that Sophia had received a letter? She cleared her throat before responding. "No, I haven't heard from him yet."

The lie startled her. Why was she lying? It was so unlike her.

"I will let you know should I hear from him, Mama... But if you'll excuse me, I will lie down for a spell. I am suddenly quite tired. I expect I am still feeling the effects of my morning ride."

Sophia excused herself and then went to her room. She closed the doors behind her carefully after entering her room. Why was she hiding this from her mother? Mama liked Henry. Everyone did.

She opened her wardrobe and took out a wooden box set with tiny emerald stones. She lifted the lid. The box's interior had red velvet lining, but nothing was inside. She had been saving this box for some special occasion, little knowing that the first thing to go into the box would be Henry's letter.

She wanted to keep this fine box a secret from Henry, too, because that would be too embarrassing. Even though he said he would be holding her own letters in a box, she couldn't think they could possibly mean the same to him as they already did to her.

She was sure he was far too busy to even think about her romantically. She would have to guard her feelings. She would write to her dear, dear friend and dream. It was all she could do.

CHAPTER 5

Let Us Be Men

My dear Jackson,

How are your studies at Eton going? I am sure you have learned much, and I hope you are keeping yourself healthy.

I wanted to give you a quick update on my life here in Paris. Rainy days seem made for delays, and I am weary of the routing. All the same, I somehow manage to cope with it all. I arise early, don my uniform to go out for early marches and weapons practice. As the days proceed, practice grows more challenging and complex, for we are learning more complicated drills alongside many studies of military strategy. Still, I have trained myself to enjoy this phase of my life.

Thankfully, our Sundays are our own to do with as we please; I read books and still enjoy riding out with my fellow batchmates. On occasion, we visit the cafes. Paris has much to offer in the way of amusement. I find society here quite different from that of London.

Today is Sunday; otherwise, I would not be writing to you. I never thought life would become so filled with so many rigorous demands. It does not seem long since we were sitting under our tent that fateful night, and then boom! With the suddenness of a cannon, all has changed. Now we are writing each other letters as adults.

I received a letter from Sophia telling me she is doing well. She informed me that you had mentioned me in your letters to her. Thank you for considering me. I sometimes miss having you by my side. I regularly reminisce about our time together and the freedoms we enjoyed. We are no longer children, though, are we? Indeed, we must focus upon our futures, n'est-ce pas?

I am looking forward to hearing from you about your experiences at Eton.

Kind Regards,

Henry.

~

Dear Henry,

Thank you for your letter. I am enjoying my stay at Eton thus far. I agree with you that our lives have become very different, and confess my studies are giving me a hard time. Learning new things has never been easy for me, the way it always did for you. I miss home, and it's been a very long time since I last visited the Estate. Thankfully we are on Holiday soon, and I eagerly anticipate the carriage ride back to Brighton.

All the same, my studies are going very well though, usually, I study at night when those around me are sleeping. I find myself needing these hours when the whole town is sleeping and the world around me is free from distraction, that I might concentrate adequately. Without these efforts, I fear I would not manage to stay abreast of my classmates, who seem so much cleverer than I.

I sometimes wonder why we do not walk away from such pursuits altogether. Would it not be more amusing to purchase a parcel of land in Brighton and build houses for ourselves there on the water, side by side? This way we would always live together, and we shall not have to write each other letters. Alas, I am being foolish. We shall blame the late hour and too much Latin, which muddles the mind.

As you well know, I am not much for letter-writing, but for you, my dear brother in everything but blood, anything. Now that I think about it, Sophia is of the age where she will soon be married to some Duke and be long gone. She would not be able to share our beach house. But I expect it shall be fine, as long as the two of us are side by side.

I am glad that your training is going well. I just know you are going *to be well-prepared for future endeavours. I expect you to become quite the hero someday.*

    All the best,

    Jackson.

Henry tossed the letter angrily onto his bed, slightly offended by Jackson's letter. He talked so casually of his sister's marriage someday. Jackson was too naïve to understand that Henry might have feelings for his sister.

In truth, Henry was quite disturbed by it all. He told himself to forget what Jackson had said. He sat out on the balcony of his sister's house.

His balcony offered a view of the bustling street below. It was almost always crowded because it was the primary market for the locals. As he looked down over the people coming and going in the busy street market below, he tried to calm his nerves.

From his vantage point, he saw a young couple buying fruit. They looked at each other adoringly, very much in love, unafraid to show the world their passion. The couple made him think of him and Sophia. He was confused about whether he should express his feelings for her or not.

What would she think of him if he did? What if she started to hate him and never wrote to him again? He could not bear to lose her friendship. What if she had already found someone else? He asked himself all these things, his mind racing.

He desperately wanted to pour his heart out to her and ask for her hand in marriage. He was obsessed with the idea, pacing the balcony, his hand on his neck, his mind trying its best to figure things out.

Henry realised he had to know how Sophia felt, whatever that cost. He would write.

CHAPTER 6

Twin Hearts

Sophia was awakened by loud noises coming from downstairs. She got up and, even though she was still in her nightgown, rushed down to see what was going on. Immediately, all the noises suddenly made sense. Jackson was home for the first time in a very long time. Mama and Papa, and all the household staff, were excitedly gathered around in the hall to welcome him home.

Sophia rushed to hug her twin brother. She had missed him so much since he was the only real company who kept her feeling alive and active at home. She didn't like it much when he was not around, even if she had gotten used to it. What choice did she have?

"Oh, I have missed you so much. You have no idea. I think 'tis true that twins will always be connected by some special bond that will never break," exclaimed Sophia.

"Oh yes, sister, we do share the same heart," Jackson winked at her. "Make sure to create a list of all the things you want to do while I am here since I am a bit short on time. I shall be going back soon enough."

She was almost in tears at the thought that her dear brother could be going back so soon.

"Oh, you should check the post," Jackson said casually. "I passed the boy on my way here."

As soon as she heard these words from Jackson, her heart skipped a beat. She was scared, confused, and excited. Part of her wanted to scream. The other wanted to cry happy tears, all at the same time. She couldn't even be sure if Henry had written to her. She had no idea so many emotions could exist in any one human at any one time. But still, she hoped.

She sent the butler to check for a letter, and when he returned, her gaze fell directly on the missives in his hand. She grabbed all of them in the most unladylike of ways before rifling through to find the one with her name on it.

She looked at the letter with a broad smile on her face for a solid minute and handed the rest of the letters back to the servant, whose face was implacable.

Thankfully Jackson was still talking about his experiences, and the family's whole attention was on him. Sophia rushed to her bedroom and locked the door behind her.

She tore apart the envelope and quickly opened the letter and read.

Dearest Sophia,

I shall give you a firm warning before you read this letter: I shall spill all the contents of my heart out upon the page, and after reading it, I hope I shall not have changed your opinion of me for ill. So, shall we begin?

When we were children, I always thought of you as my dearest friend ... until now. I do not know how I ought to react to this change in my feelings for you, but I hope you understand. Moving here, away from you, made me aware of emotions I never knew existed, or perhaps I did not wish to admit. In any case, I have feelings for you.

Your letter has warmed my heart. I find my fondness for you increasing daily. Nay, not fondness, but affection. I cannot foretell the outcome of my admission, but I surely do not wish to lose your friendship. Tell me I have not been hasty in expressing my feelings.

In his last letter, Jackson mentioned that he would be visiting home soon, so I assume he will be there by the time this letter arrives.

He also mentioned that you're moving towards the age where you are likely to consider marriage. I was unprepared for the storm of emotions I felt upon reading those words as I realised how unsettled I was by the idea of you being married to another man. I confess, I entirely lost my temper, deciding I must write you a letter. A love letter or however you may call it, Sophia.

If it were within my power, I would leave everything and come to kneel in front of you right now, begging you to be mine, to marry me and become my bride. If my words were not enough to convince you, perhaps my eyes could tell you the truth of my feelings for you. You would have seen it all in my eyes, for how could I possibly hide the love I hold for you? I would tell you that I want you more than I want anything, Sophia. I want you with all my heart, forever and always.

I cannot say these words to you, as I am here and you are there, with a great sea between us. But consider this letter my heartfelt plea to you.

I want you, Sophia. I want you, and I will always want you each day, till death parts us. Did I risk too much by saying these things to you too soon? I hope you feel the same way about me, but I will respect your decision should you say no.

I close with this thought: If you want to be with me, I will consider myself the luckiest man alive. Your love will always keep me happy. I hereby promise I would set you above anything – even the military, should you ask it. But if you decide to reject my proposal, I will never approach you again to spare you any future embarrassment.

I hope and pray I receive a positive response from you. I will always wait for your reply, no matter how long it may take you. Think this over and take your time. I will always keep you safe within my heart.

You are in my thoughts. Take care, my darling Sophia.

Love, Henry.

The ink was dripping from the letter, and Sophia quickly placed it on her dressing table, dabbing the wet ink with a dry cotton cloth. She didn't want to erase phrases from the only letter that meant the world to her. Those were her tears making it wet.

Nothing had ever made her cry tears of joy, tears of pure, pure, unadulterated happiness. She couldn't stop crying. At that moment, she wanted to run to Paris and wanted to have Henry hold her in his strong arms and weep while her head rested on his broad chest.

"Oh Henry, what have you done to me?" murmured Sophia to herself.

She looked at herself in the mirror and smiled. Suddenly, there was a knock at her door.

"Who is it?" she quickly wiped the tears from her eyes.

"It is your twin. Come down. We are waiting for you in the drawing-room to join us for tea," said Jackson.

"Yes, I am getting dressed. I shall join you in a minute. Thank you."

Sophia quickly put the letter in the box and hid it under her clothes. She washed her face to erase any signs of her having been crying, and in a short time, she was sitting enjoying breakfast with her family.

Everyone seemed happy, but Sophia was positively radiant. The happiest she had ever been. There was no way to hide the blush from her cheeks; she didn't want anyone to know her secrets yet. It wouldn't go down well with Henry leaving the military, for surely, she would ask him to do so, that she might always have him by her side.

Mama and Papa probably thought she was only smiling because Jackson was back.

CHAPTER 7

Ah...l'Amour!

Dear Henry,

It's been weeks since you moved to Paris. Time is flying by quickly, and with each passing day, I miss your presence more and more. Sometimes I wonder what you look like now? Do you have a beard? Have you grown taller? Are you still at all as you were before you left?

I expect I am much the same, at least so I think. My hair has grown a bit longer; I am a trifle taller—small changes, which likely would pass unnoticed even under close inspection.

I waited for weeks for you to write me a letter because I was too afraid to initiate correspondence with you. The truth is, I had been feeling something in my heart about you, but I never confronted those feelings until you left for France. Reading your letter brought tears to my eyes. I have never felt happier in my entire life. Your letter made me feel so loved. I am quite sure no one is ever going to love me the way you do.

You said the most perfect things at the most perfect times, as Mama has been busy seeking a match for me. I have been panicked by her efforts, for it was not only you who had these feelings. I fell in love with you too. I cannot precisely recall when or how this happened, but I guess a few things came naturally with time.

Sometimes I wish you were near, we would ride our horses on the beach, or we could sit in silence, simply holding hands watching the waves *rolling in and out from France. As for me, I watch them alone, and I think of you perhaps looking out across the water towards where I am standing.*

I would very much like to be your wife, Henry. It would be a dream come true for me. I know how much you will love me and take care of me. I would never trust anyone in my life more than you.

Both of us can make a very happy life together, full of joy and pleasure. Of course, we might expect our share of trials, but one thing I know for sure is that we are stronger than anything which could come against us, facing such difficulties with patience and composure.

And one of those necessary trials would be you leaving the military before the right time. I know your family have made considerable sacrifices, including your dear sister and her fine husband, Major Fitzsimmons. I dread to be the source of much friction, so I beg you to remain in your training until the due time. Then we can be wed.

You are always in my thoughts, Henry. In the meantime, I eagerly await your arrival with all my heart.

I put all my trust in you, Henry, well aware that you won't harm me, you won't shatter my faith, and you won't leave me alone in this world.

Be mine, as I am already yours.

Love, Sophia.

Henry couldn't believe what he had just read. He was the first-ever love letter he ever received from Sophia and unquestionably the finest love letter any man could receive. Her letter brought tears to his eyes. He craved her presence so severely that he shut his eyes and took deep breaths imagining how she looked when writing this letter. Would she have had her hair up in the current style, or would it have cascaded down her back, tied with only a ribbon in the old way? He had no idea, but he knew she looked beautiful either way.

They were so in love and counted the days until they would be reunited. The lovebirds kept on with their tradition of writing letters and storing them for the future.

CHAPTER 8
Love Endures

F*our years later*

Henry had completed his training in France and returned to London for a visit before heading to the naval academy. He couldn't wait to see Sophia. She would be in London for the Season.

Sophia was waiting for Henry to return and officially ask for her hand in marriage. The couple wanted to be married as soon as possible but knew that would be challenging. No one knew about the two of them as they agreed to keep their love a secret. They wanted to keep things private between them until they could marry.

Meanwhile, Sophia's mother was concerned about her daughter's constant disinterest in any fine gentlemen she'd thus far introduced her to and getting most exasperated. Many well-titled Lords had expressed their interest in Sophia. Sophia would have none of them.

Sophia had been very enthusiastic in preparing for the Season. She was wearing a pastel blue silk dress with a delicate pearl neckline. It was a beautiful dress with puffy sleeves, which she wore with long gloves. She matched the dress with silk shoes underneath, creating a delicate and almost ethereal presentation. She wanted to make sure she was the most beautiful girl Henry had ever laid eyes upon when he saw her that night.

Henry arrived in time for the dinner her parents had arranged in her honour, for her coming out ball.

She pinched her cheeks to bring a touch of colour into them and headed downstairs. She could hear the clinking of teacups and plates, sounds muted by the music. She was nervous. She was confused. She didn't know how to stop the shivers running down her spine. She was going to meet Henry after such a long time. Would he really feel the same when he saw her?

Everyone's eyes were on Sophia as soon as she entered the room. She didn't dare look up though she knew Henry was there. She could feel his eyes on her. She greeted everyone and then sat on the empty chair opposite to where she knew Henry was to be seated.

She was sitting directly in front of Henry. She wanted to look at him so badly. She slowly lifted her eyes from her lap and worked her way up to meet his eyes. She gasped. His eyes were already fixed on her. Like it would be a sin to take them off her. Like there was nobody else in the room. Like he had all the right to claim her. Like he was not afraid of what anyone else must be thinking.

She could feel his gaze on her body as if he was touching her. Her eyes filled up, and she had the sudden urge to hold him close and cry. She could not, of course. It would not be proper. Instead, she kept on sitting with everyone else, joining in on the polite conversation they were having about the weather.

Jackson was also home, so thankfully, he took Henry out after the meal, the gentlemen retiring to the library for brandy and cigars. The room was filled only with ladies again. She couldn't believe this handsome man was going to be her husband, her future, and the father of her children. She had never been so excited and nervous before.

On his way out, Henry handed a small letter to the maid and told her to give it to Sophia. Below was written the address and time of where they could meet in private. Sophia couldn't stop smiling as she slipped the letter into her sleeve before anyone else could see it.

That night, she wore a black hooded shawl and waited for everyone at home to be asleep. She crept out through the kitchen door. Henry was waiting for her in the herb garden beside her house. When Henry saw her coming, he ran towards her, took the lantern from her hand, and put it on the ground. He pulled her close without saying a word. As if he would never let her out of his sight.

They separated, and Sophia was blushing. She didn't even have enough courage to look him in the eyes. Henry put a finger under her chin and tilted her face in his direction.

"Hello, Sophia." He spoke her name with confidence, as if he owned it and as if he had complete control over it.

She sighed deeply, breathing slowly, taking in great gulps of air until her heart calmed and her hands steadied. Her name had never felt so strong and meaningful before.

"Hello, Henry." Her voice was shy. She was blushing. How could she be so scared and nervous at the same time? She darted glances at him, barely daring to look at him directly.

He smiled, and his eyes were gleaming. They both were hopelessly and helplessly in love. They had waited for years for this day to come. And yet here it was. And it was every bit as good as she imagined, and then some.

The next morning, Sophia woke up and got dressed as usual. But everything was not usual. Everyone was preparing for the Sunningdale ball. After all this time, Henry, Jackson, and Sophia would finally attend a ball together.

Sophia had sent Henry a letter beforehand, and they met under a bridge that afternoon. Sophia was crying hysterically. Henry reached for her, trying to calm her down, and he was confused and scared.

"Mother will not wait any longer; I know that. She has tried to match me so many times before, and I am afraid I will not be able to say no to any decision she makes for me. Henry, we have to do something. I don't want to live a life where you will be absent. I want you every day, and if I am to marry, it has to be you and not someone else," sobbed Sophia.

He didn't say anything at first. It hurt Henry everywhere to see her cry. It was the first time he saw a woman cry over him, and he didn't like a bit of it. He put his hands on her shoulders and gently pulled her close. He was holding back tears too. At that very moment, Henry realised how hard love could be.

"Sophia. You love me so much. I need you to put complete trust in me. I am going to announce things properly. Give me a day or two. I want only you. I will not see you marry someone else. I will talk to your family. I will convince them to accept my suit. After all, I am sure they like me. You are worrying yourself unnecessarily. I beg you not to cry so much as a single tear more will break my heart. Hold securely to the knowledge of my love for you."

Gently stroking her hair, Henry assured her that everything was going to be fine and that he'd make things right.

CHAPTER 9

In The Family

"How can you do that behind my back, Sophia? How can you be so selfish? Have you not thought about the gossips that will be having a field day in this town!" Mama paced the drawing-room back and forth, her hand on her forehead.

"But Mother, what is so wrong about marrying the one I love? Henry is a reputable man from a reputable family. I thought you liked him. I mean, what is there not to like? He has always respected me and has never hurt me."

Her tone was apologetic and fearful. She was afraid that everything would end, for her mother had proven to have objections to the match.

All the most important members of the Ton from Sunningdale and Brighton would be present at the New Year's ball. Every young Gentleman and Lady would attend the ball. Sophia's mother knew just how prestigious some of those Gentlemen might be and was not about to let Sophia settle for Henry when she might have so much more. At least to her way of thinking.

Of course, Henry's and Sophia's families were quite compatible. That's why Sophia's sister had married Henry's brother in the first place. Sophia couldn't understand her mother's objections. Perhaps the secrecy was the primary source of her mother's anxiety. Suppose the family would be accused of scandal even though nothing inappropriate had ever happened. In that case, some fine tittle-tattle could be written in the town's gossip columns.

The whole purpose of marriage was to provide his wife with all the necessities like food, shelter, and children. Henry was quite capable of providing her with all of that and much more. She was sure they both would make the happiest couple, and everyone in town would approve of the match. If only her mother would!

Henry was the type of man every woman wanted because he was handsome and charming. Thanks to the military for teaching him etiquette, he was also elegant and well-mannered.

On the other hand, Sophia was one of the most beautiful girls the town of Brighton had ever seen. Her eyes were deep blue, and when she smiled, her teeth were shown to be perfectly aligned. Her nose and lips, everything was in perfect shape as if God had blessed her with these special features.

Sophia wondered what reactions were arising from Henry's family. She decided to ask him about it all at the ball.

Sophia took special care with her appearance for the ball. Everyone in the room could not take their eyes off of her. She was beautifully dressed in a creamy white gown set with soft pink stones upon the bodice. Her sleeves were tight and long, and her hair was arranged, parted in the middle, and curled in gentle wisps which framed her face, the rest pulled back in soft loops pinned up at the back. One could keep looking at her forever and not tire of the beautiful sight.

Her eyes were searching for only one person: Henry. When she spotted her sister drinking punch with her husband, she went over and greeted them. The first question to fall out of her mouth was, "Will Henry be joining us today?"

She could tell from their reaction that the news was out in the family about her and Henry, and no one was happy about it. Sophia swallowed hard as if something was stuck in her throat. Their lacklustre response did not bode well. She retreated to the ballroom, where many gentlemen were seen mingling with the ladies.

And there he was, handsome-looking Henry. She smiled when she saw him. Henry hadn't noticed her yet, and she gave him an intense look as though she feared never seeing him again. She'd never seen a man looking so handsome as he did now.

Henry caught her looking at him and started to make his way towards her. Every muscle in her body tightened, and she started blushing, looking down at her feet. He held her hand and cradled it in his hand, carefully, delicately.

"Would you like to have a dance with me, Miss Sophia?" inquired Henry, already drawing her towards the other dancers.

"I would like that, yes," replied Sophia.

Every time Henry called out her name, something in her tightened. She felt wondrous things every time he addressed her.

Both of them bowed, then started to dance. All eyes were on this beautiful couple. Not everyone was pleased with the match, she saw. There was much jealousy in their looks.

No, not everyone was upset. Sophia heard more than one kind word and saw more than a few smiles.

"They would make such beautiful children," someone said.

"I think it's true," Henry whispered in Sophia's ear, which made her smile as well.

"Henry, how are things with your family?" asked Sophia.

"Sophia, you are going to be my wife. I cannot, and I will not ever let you go. You can mark my words. You're worth the fight. I will fight for you till my last dying breath."

His face was severe. He had claimed her, and now her heart was forever in his control.

"I love you, Henry." A tear rolled down her cheek, and Henry brushed it away with his finger. "I can waste not one more minute!"

Henry turned abruptly, interrupting the dance, and marched straight towards Sophia's parents, who were watching. "Lord and Lady Barrington. Sophia and I have been best friends for years, and love bloomed, making its way to us. Is it so bad for such friends to fall in love? ... Surely this is the basis for a good marriage?"

He looked around the ballroom. "Forget what the gossips might say! I assure you here, and now, nothing untoward has ever happened between us... A man provides for his family and looks after his wife. For Sophia, I am willing to do so much more than that. You can order me anything, any single thing, and I shall do it. I have no greater honour than to serve her. I value her happiness more than mine, more than anyone else's. I would not see her worry or stand her pain. I want to make her the happiest. I want to be with her for every single minute for the rest of our lives.

"She is the most beautiful woman I have ever seen in Paris or Brighton or Sunningdale. She is my best friend, and I want her to be my wife more than I want anything.

"Even though I say these words out loud, my heart is trembling, and fear still resides in it: the fear of losing her. I am a soldier. Not once have I feared a bullet. But I fear this. I love her with all my heart, and I will never stop doing that. Never. And so, I beg you not to make us wait any longer," said Henry.

A stream of tears could be seen falling from Sophia's eyes, and in no time, she was stifling sobs. She couldn't stop crying. They had utterly put her fate into her parents' hands and were waiting for their reply.

"I don't think anyone will ever love me the way Henry does," she said, wiping away her tears. "And no one will ever love Henry more than I do."

A tear rolled down her Papa's cheek. "You have my permission to marry my daughter."

Right there in the ballroom, Henry knelt and made it official, asking Sophia to marry him. Of course, she said yes in front of the whole of Brighton.

They were sitting in the drawing-room at Sunningdale Manor when Jackson brought up the topic of the wedding and the preparations.

"I will have to go back home to deal with Estate business. Let us start making arrangements before that. I want to share in your joy. My sister and best friend are betrothed. I could not be happier," he said.

"I would not want you to miss a moment. I will make sure of it," replied Henry.

Every time Henry looked at her, she blushed and looked away. Henry was quite impressed that she was too shy to even hold his gaze for longer than five seconds. Even now, when they were officially promised to each other.

"Oh Sophia, you shall soon be my wife. The mother of my children. They will grow up to thank me for choosing such a loving, caring, and beautiful mother for them as you. If only I could hold you in my arms right now and tell you how beautiful you look." Henry whispered the words so that only Sophia could hear them.

Sophia looked around. Everyone else was busy chattering about the wedding preparations and enjoying tea, and no one but her had heard.

They only saw the young and handsome couple, so head over heels in love with one another that they could not wait to walk down the aisle.

Epilogue

Preparations were going on for the marriage, and the town was extremely happy for the young couple. There had been no negative tittle-tattle about what they assumed was such a speedy courtship, which both families were highly relieved about.

Most people assumed Henry had fallen in love with Sophia at the ball, as if seeing her with fresh eyes for the first time, and this is what they let people think was the case. She had looked so charming that night, so it was believable that such a handsome young officer could be so smitten to propose to her on the first night.

They were to be married in Spring, which was just a month away, and everyone was busy preparing for the marriage. They were to be married in a church with their loved ones by their side. They wanted to invite everyone to join them on this special occasion and start the new journey of their life with lots of prayers and support.

Sophia and Henry continued their tradition of writing each other letters – love letters. Their love was growing deeper and stronger with each passing day. When everyone was asleep at night, they sometimes crept out of the house and sat in silence on the beach and listened to the sound of the waves crashing on the shore.

And now, finally, their wedding day had arrived. It was a day that they felt they had been waiting for their entire life.

Sophia wore the most beautiful dress anyone had ever seen. Creamy white and covered in heavy lace, her gown was exquisite. Her veil was of lace, and she wore the finest of pearl earrings and a matching pearl necklace. All of this made her look even more beautiful. She wore long silk gloves to match.

Everyone was seated and waiting for Sophia to enter the church. Everyone rose when she entered. They gasped when they saw her. She was radiant with happiness.

She entered the church with a fragrant white rose bouquet in her right hand and her left hand tied around Jackson's arm. Someone had thought to place extra flowers about, white roses, enough to create a bower. It was just how she wanted her big day to be.

Her face was covered with a lacy veil. Henry waited patiently as she inched her way down the aisle.

Henry closed his eyes for a second when he saw her. She was looking more beautiful than ever. She was looking heavenly, unreal. He could hardly believe she was truly his.

As the service progressed, the Priest motioned to Henry that he could now put the ring on her finger. He took out a red velvet box from the inside of his coat. He held Sophia's hand and removed the glove, looking straight into her eyes. Sophia was trembling all over and felt like she could hardly breathe.

He placed the ring on her ring finger, and it was the most beautiful jewel anyone had ever seen. She gasped at the sight of the beautiful ring. Henry indeed has taken his time to search for the right one.

They both read their vows out loud, and finally, they heard what they were waiting for. What they had waited over four years, and perhaps their whole young lives, to hear.

"In the name of the Father, the Son, and the Holy Ghost, I now pronounce you man and wife."

Smiles were seen everywhere. It was as if their marriage had given Brighton a new lease on life. After the wedding, there was a party, and everyone from the town and country joined them for this special occasion.

It was a lovely sight to see a handsome couple achieve so much in such a short time, they all said. Perhaps their love was more potent than most, and they knew how to love the right way. But these townsfolk didn't know the half of it.

Henry and Sophia were constantly seen sharing eye contact and smiles throughout the whole day, both having a hard time taking their eyes off each other. How beautifully in love they were, everyone said. Their future was theirs to make.

During a quiet moment, Henry handed his new bride a letter he had written for her. "Here's one for your collection," he whispered.

She opened it and read:

My darling, beautiful wife,
Words fail me today to describe how beautiful you look. So I will just say I am yours forever. When words fail, love takes over, and love has taken hold of me now.
Your loving husband,
Henry

Many more letters would follow over the years that they, their children, and grandchildren would cherish forever.

The End
Did you enjoy *The Allington Collection*?
Please consider rating it on <u>Goodreads</u>, <u>Bookbub</u> or your favorite retailer. Reviews help me reach new readers.

Read **The Gillingham Collection**, the next collection in The Lady Series.

Join my Newsletter for updates, sales and giveaways!

Glossary of Regency Terms

Adventuress – a woman of loose morals, wild

Almack's - Private, very exclusive balls were held there each Wednesday night of the Season. Only those approved by the patronesses were allowed to attend.

Apoplexy – a fit

Bag of moonshine - a lot of nonsense

Bit of muslin - a woman of easy virtue

Blue devilled - depressed

Bounder - a man of objectionable social behaviour

Cad - a man who doesn't treat women proper.

Canterbury tales - lies.

Chatelaine – the keeper of the keys, ruler about who went where

Chit - a saucy, forward girl

Coming Out – A young lady's first entry into Society. Presented first at the Royal Court to the ruling monarch, a ball was later held in her honour. She is hereafter free to attend social events and seek a husband.

Countenance - a person's face or facial expression

Dalliance – courtship, relationship

Dash it – to Hell with it

Devil's own scrape – terrible trouble

Devil to pay - trouble
Doing it much too brown - overdoing it so that it is not credible
Dressing down – telling off
Flush in the pockets - rich
Fustian – rubbish, nonsense
Gammon - lie or nonsense
Get on – manage, run
High dudgeon - very angry
Hogwash – nonsense, rubbish
Hoyden – A mischievous, spunky girl who is felt to lack decorum.
Incomparable - a female of the ton without rival, match or peer.
Kick up a lark – get up to mischief
Libertine - a person, especially a man, who freely indulges in sensual pleasures without regard to moral principles
Loose in the haft - has many vices and little respect for proprieties
Make a cake of oneself - make a fool of self
Not a feather to fly with - to have no money
Not care a fig – not care at all
Purse-pinched - have little money
Raising a breeze – up to mischief
Reticule – handbag
Ride roughshod over – bend to your will
Riding habit – the clothes women wore for riding; a skirt, jacket, hat, boots and often gloves
Romp – fun, joke
Shockingly loose in the haft - has many vices and little respect for proprieties.
Stirrup-cups – shot of alcohol to keep riders warm
Toilette - outfit
Ton – high Society
To go about – to behave
To be a goose – be silly
Throwing a rub in the way - spoiling the plans